"I'm going to keep you safe, Laney."

"I'm certainly not going to let anybody run me out of town. Not when we have a job to do."

His lips tilted into a smile. She'd always been the strongest person he knew—maybe ten years hadn't changed *everything*.

A couple of minutes later, he pulled the car under the canopy outside the hotel and shut off the engine. Laney opened her door and climbed out.

He chewed the inside of his lip for a moment. "Do you feel comfortable staying here, after what happened?"

"I'll be fine." She flashed her cell phone. "The police department is only a phone call away."

He set the suitcase off to the side and closed the trunk. "I know, but—"

Their only warning was a sudden, sharp hissing noise from the suitcase. Adrenaline flooded his system and he yanked Laney's arm, smacking her into the back of the car as he flung himself between her and the bag.

The suitcase exploded.

Kellie VanHorn is an award-winning author of inspirational romance and romantic suspense. She has college degrees in biology and nautical archaeology, but her sense of adventure is most satisfied by a great story. When not writing, Kellie can be found homeschooling her four children, camping, baking and gardening. She lives with her family in western Michigan.

Books by Kellie VanHorn

Love Inspired Suspense

Fatal Flashback
Buried Evidence

Visit the Author Profile page at Harlequin.com.

BURIED
EVIDENCE

KELLIE VANHORN

LOVE INSPIRED SUSPENSE
INSPIRATIONAL ROMANCE

LOVE INSPIRED® SUSPENSE
INSPIRATIONAL ROMANCE

ISBN-13: 978-1-335-55446-8

Recycling programs
for this product may
not exist in your area.

Buried Evidence

Copyright © 2021 by Kellie VanHorn

This edition published by arrangement with Harlequin Books S.A.

For questions and comments about the quality of this book, please contact us at CustomerService@Harlequin.com.

Love Inspired
22 Adelaide St. West, 40th Floor
Toronto, Ontario M5H 4E3, Canada
www.Harlequin.com

Printed in U.S.A.

Because he hath set his love upon me,
therefore will I deliver him: I will set him on high,
because he hath known my name.
—*Psalm* 91:14

For those who have suffered
the long-lasting pain of ambiguous loss.

With my unending appreciation to my agent Ali Herring,
my editor Dina Davis, and my critique partners
Michelle Keener and Kerry Johnson,
who all helped shape this book into a story
worth reading, and also for my family—
I wouldn't be an author without your love and support.

ONE

Laney Hamilton couldn't shake the feeling she was being followed.

Adjusting the leather strap of her messenger bag, she glanced over her shoulder as she walked down the regional airport's long ramp leading to the baggage claim on the lower level. Only the same handful of ticketed passengers who'd shared the bumpy flight from Indianapolis trailed behind her. The plane had been tiny—the kind with just one seat on each side of the aisle—and aside from the harried mother dragging along her infant and screaming toddler, everyone kept to themselves.

Maybe the jitters came from being back here in southern Indiana again, ten years after she'd shaken the proverbial dust off her boots and sworn never to return. Or maybe it was knowing who might be waiting with the squad car to drive her back to her hometown of Sandy Bluff.

Lord, please let it be anyone but *Ryan Mitchell.*

A decade hadn't been long enough to erase the memory of his broken expression when she'd told him she was leaving.

Which was just stupid, considering they'd been only

teenagers. As if a pair of eighteen-year-olds could make a relationship work for a lifetime.

At the bottom of the ramp, she spotted a sign for the ladies' room. She'd better take a moment to freshen up and make sure she didn't appear as frazzled as she felt. The heavy door swung shut on silent hinges as she slipped inside one of the stalls. Hopefully whoever the police chief sent would wait outside the terminal, giving her a few extra minutes to mentally prepare. Of course, half a day's worth of travel from Washington, DC, hadn't been enough, so maybe that was wishful thinking.

A latch clicked shut somewhere inside the bathroom, startling Laney out of her thoughts. Another one of the passengers, no doubt. She glanced around the space as she stepped up to the sink to wash her hands but didn't see anyone.

Time to get this over with. Letting out a tense sigh, she stuck her hands beneath the dryer. Hot air blasted over her skin like a tornado.

As she pulled her hands back and the noise died, something hard and sharp pricked the center of Laney's back. *A knife?* Her heart skyrocketed into her throat, but before she could call for help or think through the haze of panic, a low, muffled voice spoke. Male or female, she couldn't tell.

"Don't move and don't make a sound. I know why you're here. Get on the next flight and leave now, or you won't get another chance. Now count to fifty."

Laney sucked in a few rapid breaths and started counting. "One, two, three…" The knife point disappeared from her back, followed by barely audible footfalls.

Should she risk turning around? Curiosity won by the time she reached fifteen. She kept saying the numbers aloud but pivoted on her foot, glancing around the bathroom. The tile floor was empty, leading past the bank of sinks and mirrors and vanishing around a corner into another section of stalls. In the distance, a soft *whumph* sounded—her attacker leaving through a second exit.

Drawing in a shaky breath, Laney turned to the door she'd entered. The latch had been flipped shut, locking it from the inside—the click she'd heard. She jerked it open and escaped into the freedom of the airport's corridor, then darted past the restroom to glance down an adjoining hallway. Surely the exit had led out here, but there was no sign of her attacker.

Time to find security.

No one was in sight, so she dashed through the sliding doors into the baggage claim area. One of the conveyer belts had started up, and passengers from her flight gathered around it, waiting for their bags. An airport security guard stood nearby.

Relief fluttered through Laney's chest as she dashed up to him and spilled out her story like a soda falling off an airplane-tray table. His brown eyebrows pinched together, but he pulled out his radio immediately and rattled off a series of commands.

"If you're okay, ma'am, I'm going to check that restroom."

She nodded, tucking a few strands of her short dark hair back behind her ear. "Thank you."

"Wait here. I'll need you to fill out a report."

The man disappeared back through the sliding doors, and Laney held her breath, wishing the glass wasn't frosted. After a couple of minutes in which nothing happened, she glanced over at the nearby moving conveyer belt.

Bags had started lurching their way up out of the

murky depths of the cargo area and now dropped onto the belt. She kept an eye out for her black Samsonite carry-on, watching as one passenger after another claimed a suitcase and retreated through the doors toward the parking lot.

She'd packed light for this trip. Lieutenant James Mitchell, Ryan's father and chief of the Sandy Bluff police, had assured her they needed her expertise for only a few days. As a postdoctoral fellow in the Physical Anthropology Department of the Smithsonian, Laney was used to assisting local law enforcement with forensic analysis of human remains, but southern Indiana wasn't exactly local.

Not anymore.

But when she'd asked Jim why he wanted *her* out of all the forensic anthropologists available, he'd merely said, *You're the right one for this case, Laney. We need you here.*

If it had been anybody else asking her to come back here, she would've said no. Too busy with work. Too many other cases. Too many projects to complete if she was going to make a name for herself among the stellar staff of the Smithsonian.

She grimaced as the last of the passengers plucked a bag off the conveyer belt and it groaned to a halt. Great. No suitcase. A quick glance at her phone showed no word from her ride yet either.

A few minutes later, the frosted doors slid open and the security guard returned, claiming her attention. The downturn to his lips didn't bode well.

"I'm sorry, ma'am," he said as he walked up to her. "We couldn't find any trace of your attacker. We'll get someone looking at the security footage, though."

Laney swallowed. Jim hadn't said much about the case, but he *had* mentioned wanting to keep her arrival quiet.

Apparently it was too late for that. A little chill tracked down her spine as she followed the security guard to his workstation, where she recounted the story one more time. The laptop keys clicked away under his fingers as he entered the details.

After assuring her they'd be in touch, the guard escorted her back to the now-desolate baggage claim area. "Anything else I can do for you, ma'am?"

Laney glanced back at the empty belt that had conveyed the bags from her flight. They'd checked her carry-on at the gate in Indianapolis because the tiny plane's overhead bins were too cramped. She'd wheeled it to the end of the boarding ramp herself. How could it not have made it on the plane? "As a matter of fact, my bag didn't arrive. Can you direct me to the baggage claim office?"

He pointed past the silent conveyer belts. "I'd better escort you down there myself."

Laney smiled gratefully. Her heels clicked on the concrete floor as they walked past the belts toward the office at the far end of the hall. A glance out the exit sliders as they passed showed only an empty loading area.

Where was her ride? As soon as she took care of the luggage problem, she'd text Jim. Find out what was going on. Because texting Ryan was going to happen *never* and she'd cut ties with all her other old friends. Her one connection left in Sandy Bluff was her mother, still living in that horrid, tumbledown trailer Laney had vowed she'd never set foot inside again. She made phone calls on Christmas and on Kim's birthday and sent occasional Facebook messages. That was it.

Ten years and she'd never visited, not once. And if she could avoid it now, all the better. No reason to traipse back down that trail of misery and regret after how hard she'd worked to escape. Some memories were better left buried and forgotten where they couldn't hurt you anymore.

Laney crinkled her nose as she peeked inside the open office door. The single desk chair was empty, the computer apparently off.

The guard stepped inside and pointed at a couple of beat-up bags bearing pink claim tickets, standing against one wall. "Is it one of those?"

"No." So much for that idea. "I guess I can go ask one of the ticketing agents."

She backed out of the doorway, her heart lurching as she collided with someone who hadn't been there a second before.

A hand gripped her elbow. Laney jerked her arm free, spinning on her heels to face a brown-haired man in gray pants and an orange safety vest.

He raised the hand that had been touching her a second before. "Sorry, ma'am. Didn't mean to startle you."

Airline employee, judging by the Delta emblem emblazoned on his uniform. She swallowed. "Of course. It was my fault." Having a burly security guard at her back made her feel a whole lot better.

"Someone missed loading this one on the belt. I'm dropping it off for baggage claim." He glanced down at a familiar black Samsonite carry-on with green luggage tags.

"It's my bag." She pressed a hand against her stomach as some of her anxiety deflated. "Thank you so much."

The man smiled, his weathered skin crinkling around hazel eyes. "Happy to help, ma'am."

She reached for the handle of the bag, expecting him to let go, but when he didn't, her fingers brushed against his hand. A chill tracked down her spine, and the man's smile deepened as something shifted in his gaze.

Like he'd recognized her. He tilted his head to one side, finally releasing the handle. "Welcome home."

As he turned away, Laney could swear he winked at her. But it *had* to be her imagination. She'd never seen him before in her life. How could he know her?

By the time she wheeled her bag out of the office, he'd melted back into the shadows.

"Are you all set now, ma'am?" her security escort asked once they reached the sliding exit doors. As he spoke, a pair of headlights turned into the loading line. Glare from the streetlights glinted red and blue off the top of the car as it rolled to a stop in front of the doors.

Her phone buzzed as a text came through, the caller ID showing a Sandy Bluff area code.

Laney, just pulling up outside.

Good. She wouldn't be trapped at this desolate airport all night.

"Yes, thank you. There's my ride."

Muggy summer air slapped her in the face as she walked out onto the sidewalk, bringing back a hundred memories of late nights swimming at the quarry and playing tag in the farmers' fields. She squeezed her eyes shut, trying to stem the flow. Ryan lurked in nearly every one of those memories, and even though she'd done her best to make her brain forget, her heart still hadn't. But as far as romance was concerned, he was absolutely out of the question. Not with the secrets she'd kept all these years.

The driver's-side door opened, and a man stepped out.

He walked around the front of the car, where the headlights revealed dark blue pants, a heavy gun belt and a blue shirt but obscured his face. His build wasn't familiar, but the voice she knew immediately.

"Hey, Laney."

She swallowed.

Jim had sent Ryan Mitchell. Only he wasn't a lanky teenager anymore, he was a man. Even with her heels on, she was a good six inches shorter than he was. And he hadn't grown only in height—his broad shoulders stretched beneath the protective vest, and the short sleeves of his uniform revealed solid muscle in his arms.

He'd been tall, dark and handsome at eighteen. Now he was model-worthy gorgeous.

She was in serious trouble.

Knowing he was here to pick up Laney Hamilton and seeing her in the flesh were very different things, Ryan decided. He'd even had a few seconds to collect himself as he pulled up to the curb, but that didn't stop him from feeling like he had two left feet as he walked up to where she stood with one hand clutching the strap of her shoulder bag and the other gripping the handle of her suitcase.

"Hi, Ryan." Her gaze swept over him, starting at his boot-clad feet and up to his head, and he couldn't help swiping a sweaty palm across his uniform.

"You cut your hair," he said, then bit the inside of his cheek. Surely he could've come up with something better.

She'd kept it long in high school, nearly reaching to

her waist. Now she wore it in a pixie cut that suited her delicate cheekbones and short stature. If he had to guess, he'd say she was still five foot three, the same height as the last time he'd seen her. Whether or not she was the same tiny firecracker remained to be seen.

She tucked a dark strand behind her ear. "Yeah. It... got in the way."

Silence stretched between them. What did you say to a former girlfriend after so many years? Especially when you'd never really moved on?

Not that he hadn't tried dating other girls. His friends took every opportunity to set him up. But no woman had captured his heart the way Laney had.

Had, being the key word there.

He'd be wise to remember that every time he thought about her. Their relationship was a thing of the distant past, and she was here only to do a job.

"Sorry I'm late," he said, throwing a thumb over his shoulder in the general direction of Sandy Bluff. "The highway's down to one lane, and the traffic was awful."

It sounded like a stupid excuse, and he regretted it the instant the words left his mouth. If this conversation was any indicator, the ride home was going to be horribly awkward. Why had he agreed to pick her up?

Oh, right. Because this was his case. Human remains had been found in the bog, east of town. He and his father had taken one look at the visible bones—stripped clean and blanched to a dull gray—and decided to leave them in place until they could bring in outside help. Choosing Laney had been his father's call, and Ryan knew exactly why.

His twin sister Jenna had vanished while on a long bicycle ride on a perfect summer day ten years ago.

The only clue they'd ever found was her bike, its frame twisted and both tires flat, a hundred yards off the road at the bottom of a long, tree-covered slope. Laney had left two months later when they'd called off the search.

And now she was back, watching him with those big brown eyes, dressed in black slacks and a jacket and heels, all grown up and more beautiful than ever.

She gave him a tight-lipped smile. "That's okay. I didn't wait too long."

He cleared his throat and opened the passenger-side door. "Here, let me get your bag."

She relinquished her grip on the rolling carry-on and slid into the passenger seat. He closed the door behind her, the movement both foreign and terrifyingly familiar at the same time. How many times had he helped her into a car like this before? And yet everything was different now. There could be no going back.

After depositing the suitcase into the car's trunk, he climbed in behind the wheel and pulled away from the airport. The drive to Sandy Bluff would take a solid thirty minutes. He needed some common ground for conversation besides their past, which she was obviously as keen to ignore as he was.

He eased the car onto the road and headed through a couple of stoplights out to the highway. It was late enough now that the traffic had dissipated and the roads were mostly empty. Darkness shrouded the surrounding hills and farm fields.

She'd always been the talkative one, and she broke the silence first. "Ryan…" She shifted uncomfortably in her seat. "Somebody attacked me in the airport bathroom."

What? Heat flooded his insides, and he gritted his teeth. He and his father knew this case would garner local attention, and any new evidence on a cold case *could* lead to danger if somebody got jumpy, but still… Letting out a slow breath, he adopted his most calm, professional tone. "Are you okay? What happened?"

She held up a hand, just visible in the dashboard lights, and turned toward him. "I'm fine, just a little rattled. It wasn't an attack, really. More of a threat that I'd be in danger if I didn't leave Indiana immediately. Airport security looked into it but couldn't find the culprit. All I can think is that someone doesn't want me on this case."

Ryan gripped the steering wheel a bit tighter. "I'm sorry, Laney. If I'd known, I would've been there to meet you at the gate."

"It's not your fault. But what's this all about? Your father told me he'd fill me in once I got here."

"Teenagers found bones in Waltman's Bog two days ago, just east of the old Clapton place." He paused, clearing his throat. *Lord, why does this have to be so hard?* There was no way to talk about their hometown without dredging up memories better left buried. He, his sister, Laney and their friends had traipsed through that same bog on more than one occasion in high school. "We found what looks like a human femur and possibly parts of a hand. Dad didn't want to dig for more until you got here."

"Were they clean?"

He nodded, his throat unexpectedly constricting. It wouldn't take long for Laney to figure out what his dad was thinking. "They look old."

Her hand went to her chest, and she turned away from the window to look at him. "Do you think…?" Her voice trailed away, and she paused for a long moment before continuing, "Do you think it could be Jenna?"

"I… Maybe. Dad thought we should bring somebody in to help collect the evidence."

"And calling me was his idea?"

Ryan nodded. "He wanted somebody familiar with the area. With our city."

With Jenna.

But had his father considered how hard this case might be on Laney? He glanced over at her. She still had her hand pressed to her chest, but her gaze had turned back to the passenger-side window. She stared out into the darkness and the intermittent lights from houses dotting the fields.

After a long moment, she pulled her hand away and tucked it with the other into her lap. He flexed his fingers on the wheel—anything to get rid of this urge to take up that slim hand into his own. The last time he'd touched her had been at the combined prayer vigil and memorial service, when she'd hugged him and said goodbye. She hadn't even been able to look him in the eye.

"Your dad warned me he wanted to keep my arrival quiet," she said. "Why?"

He let out a quick huff of air. "We've tried to keep the find as low-key as possible. Though, from the way local reporters swarmed the bog immediately, you'd think the kids called them before the cops. But it's not only because of the possible connection to Jenna's disappearance. Have you followed the news here at all since you left?" The last few words were hard to get out past the squeezing in his chest.

"I've heard a few things. More disappearances. A murder a few years ago. Mom said you caught the killer. I'd kind of hoped he was the one responsible for…" Her voice trailed away.

His sister. Maybe now, if they'd finally found her remains, they'd get answers.

"My family hoped the same. But here's the catch," he said grimly. "Ronald Wilson, the guy they pinned for three murders, didn't move to Sandy Bluff until six months after Jenna vanished. He was on an oil rig in the Gulf of Mexico before then."

She turned a sharp gaze on him. "Then you already know he didn't kill Jenna."

"Right. But without her remains, we've never been able to figure out what happened to her." His throat tightened at the thought of what Jenna might've endured. "Her death could've been accidental, like a hit-and-run. Or we could be looking at a separate murder."

"Another killer? That person might be the one trying to scare me off before we figure it out," she mused. "Or if the remains aren't hers, we might have one more victim to add to your killer's list. But then, why threaten me?"

"That brings me to something else. Wilson's been locked up in Indiana State Prison for two years, and we haven't had a disappearance since—until last week. Nineteen-year-old college girl, home for summer break. She vanished a couple days before we found the bones."

"That's awful. But if it's been less than a week, there's a chance she ran away, right?"

"We're doing a full search, of course. But all our leads have already gone cold." No family should have to endure what had happened to his. He'd joined law enforcement not only to follow in his father's footsteps but because of Jenna. And yet they'd failed to protect so many.

His heart twisted as he took the exit for Sandy Bluff and turned onto the winding, narrow road leading to the small rural town.

"What about the possibility Wilson was framed?" She shivered, then rubbed her hands over her arms. "Maybe there's still a serial killer on the loose."

"Unfortunately, that might be the case." He tightened his grip on the steering wheel. "If the remains in the bog are linked in any way to the latest disappearance or to someone with something to hide… That's why we wanted to keep your arrival secret."

"After what happened at the airport, I can see why."

"I'm going to keep you safe, Laney." He glanced at her, unable to ignore how vulnerable she seemed with her hands clasped in her lap. "You don't have to worry."

The lights from the dashboard reflected in her gaze. "I'm certainly not going to let anybody run me out of town. Not when we have a job to do."

His lips tilted into a smile. She'd always been the strongest person he knew—maybe ten years hadn't changed *everything*. The thought triggered an unexpected pang of loneliness as he stopped at a red light on the outskirts of town. Sandy Bluff's roller rink, permanently shuttered a year after Laney moved, sat forlorn and decaying to his left.

He cleared his throat. "Dad booked you at the new Hampton Inn, right?"

She pulled out her cell phone, its screen filling the car with an eerie blue glow. "Yes, I've got the reservation information here."

A couple of minutes later, he pulled the car under the canopy outside the hotel and shut off the engine. He and Laney climbed out.

He rubbed his jaw as he walked to the trunk. "Do you feel comfortable staying here after what happened?"

"I'll be fine." She flashed her cell. "The police department's only a phone call away."

After pulling out Laney's carry-on, he set it off to the side and closed the trunk. "I know, but—"

Their only warning was a sudden sharp hissing noise from the suitcase. Adrenaline flooded his system and he yanked Laney's arm, smacking her into the back of the car as he flung himself between her and the bag.

The suitcase exploded.

TWO

Laney threw her arms over her face, squeezing her eyes shut as flame and shrapnel shot across the back of the patrol car. The force of the blast threw both her and Ryan to the ground, and hard blacktop and shattered glass bit into her hands and knees through the thin fabric of her slacks. Her ears rang from the noise of the explosion.

Ryan's arm lay draped over her back like a heavy weight. She pushed up to her knees, her head throbbing, and crawled out from under him. He didn't move.

"Ryan?"

He lay on his stomach, face turned toward her, eyes closed. His back had borne the brunt of the explosion—patches of his shirt were scorched away, revealing the standard-issue flak jacket underneath.

She pressed trembling fingers against his neck, feeling for a pulse as a prayer stole swiftly from her heart. Relief flooded through her as she felt the steady throb of his heartbeat beneath her fingers.

Through the haze of smoke and burning debris, someone came running through the shattered doors of the hotel lobby. A woman, dressed in a tidy pencil skirt and blouse. Her mouth moved, but Laney couldn't hear her words.

She shook her head, the movement sending pain lancing down her neck. The woman held up a finger as if telling her to wait and pressed a cell phone to her ear. More people moved inside the lobby now—curious travelers coming to investigate the explosion.

Someone threw a blanket over Laney's shoulders, and she clutched it tightly with one hand, rocking back and forth as she crouched beside Ryan. He still hadn't stirred. She traced a finger over his cheek, noting the texture of the bristly day-old stubble and the feel of his dark hair. Soft as it had been ten years ago. As if no time had passed, and yet so much distance lay between them.

Finally a sound broke through the rushing silence in her ears—a siren. First one, then another, then another. A cop car pulled up beside theirs, followed a moment later by a fire truck and an ambulance.

Thank You, Lord. Please let Ryan be okay.

She might want to keep a lid on the past and never see him again, but she wouldn't ever wish more hurt on him. Not after everything he'd gone through already. Guilt coiled inside her stomach, but she shoved it aside. That part of her life was over.

From what her mother had told her about him going with his parents to church now, maybe he'd become a Christian too. Hopefully so—they needed all the optimism they could get in this line of work.

Footsteps pounded across the asphalt, and she recognized Ryan's father right away. Same dark crew cut, now streaked with gray, same facial features that hovered between stern and ready to laugh. Though right now he looked only worried as he dropped to the pavement on Ryan's other side. He glanced between the two of them.

"Laney?" When she nodded, he pointed at her head. "Your hair's short."

The same thing Ryan had said. She shrugged. Ryan *had* always been just like his father. No surprise he'd become a cop too.

Jim Mitchell laid a gentle hand on Ryan's shoulder. "Ryan?"

His eyelids fluttered, and Laney couldn't help letting out a little sigh of relief when his dark brown gaze focused on her face. "You okay?" he croaked.

"Still alive, thanks to you."

He started to roll onto his back but stopped, wincing in pain.

"Don't try to move, son," Jim said. He stepped aside as a pair of EMTs lowered a gurney to the ground beside Ryan. They helped him onto it, stomach down to keep the pressure off his injured back.

As they hoisted him up, Ryan pointed at Laney. "She needs to be checked out too. Do *not* let her out of your sight."

In the background, a pair of officers cordoned off the area to preserve the evidence while another spoke to the onlookers.

Jim climbed to his feet, offering Laney a hand. "Can you stand? You and I are going with him." He nodded toward the retreating EMTs. "We'll talk about what happened while they patch you two up."

Her knees protested as she got to her feet, and her right leg ached from smashing into the car, but nothing felt broken. One of the EMTs jogged up to her, taking her other elbow and guiding her toward the ambulance. She and the police chief climbed in and took seats beside

Ryan, who craned his neck to see them. "We shouldn't have dragged her into this, Dad."

Jim frowned. "If it wasn't Laney, it'd be somebody else. But how did anyone know you'd be here? And what happened?"

"They knew what flight she was on," Ryan said.

Whoever had threatened her at the airport sure hadn't wasted any time. Staring down at her palm, Laney picked at a shard of glass embedded in her skin. The blast hadn't been that big, but if she'd been closer to her suitcase when it blew…

"Stop," Jim said, pulling her hands apart. "Leave it to the professionals. Now explain."

It took only a few minutes to recount both the airport attack and the details of the explosion. "I'm just grateful I wasn't standing next to it. I could've been in the hotel elevator. Or unpacking it in the room." She sucked on her lip. "It's like whoever planted it knew how long it would take me to get here and rigged the bomb to go off right when I'd be hauling my suitcase inside."

"More likely they used a cell phone to detonate it at the exact moment they wanted," Ryan countered, his voice muffled against the stretcher.

"They were watching us?" Somehow that thought was even creepier than the bomb.

"We'll know more when we get the lab work-up," Jim said. "But how did they get it into your bag? Did you take it on the plane?"

"Yes, from Dulles to Indy. But the plane for the flight down here was too small. I checked it at the gate." She tapped her finger against her chin. "And then my bag didn't arrive. A guy rolled it up to me at the baggage claim office."

"Who?" Ryan asked. "Was it long enough it could've been the same person who threatened you?"

"Maybe twenty minutes later? He looked like an employee. The voice didn't sound the same, but that could've been intentional."

"We'll need to check the security footage," Jim said. "Both for Evansville Regional and Indianapolis."

"That's a lot of potential baggage handlers." Ryan grunted as the ambulance jolted over a bumpy stretch of pavement.

"But how many of them could have a possible connection to me or to this case?" Laney asked. And how had word gotten out about her arrival in the first place? Of course, with local reporters already on the story, it probably wasn't that unlikely.

Finally the ambulance rolled to a stop. The EMTs pulled open the rear doors and ushered Laney, Jim and Ryan inside. A nurse tended to her burns and cuts while hospital staff examined Ryan in another room. Other than some bruises and the glass fragments in her palms, she'd gotten away with relatively few injuries compared to what could've happened. She needed to thank Ryan for his quick action and the way he'd covered her to take the brunt of the explosion. That's what had saved her.

In the waiting area, Jim had already made calls to get the security footage and the names of all the airline employees who could have handled her bag. The list was daunting, but Jim shrugged.

"That's the nature of the game," he said, stowing his phone back in his pocket. "It's why we always have too many open cases and not enough manpower to solve them all. Hannah down at the precinct is already pulling files, and when you come in tomorrow, we'll go over the potential suspects."

They released Ryan an hour later, and she had to check her impulse to hug him as he walked out. Just because he'd saved her life didn't mean they could revert to the old days. She didn't *want* to do that anyway. Escaping Sandy Bluff had been the best decision she'd ever made, and she wasn't about to take it back now.

Funny how that line she'd told herself for so many years suddenly felt like a lie.

Arms clasped across her stomach, she stood back as Jim looked Ryan over. The way his eyes glistened tugged at her heart, despite her best intentions.

"Glad you're all right, son."

Ryan, now wearing only a white undershirt with his uniform pants, held up the flak jacket and blue shirt he carried draped over one arm. "I'm afraid these have seen better days. But the jacket saved me from being roasted alive."

She offered Ryan a tiny smile. "Thank you for protecting me."

Something shifted in his dark eyes, making her breath catch. "I'll always protect you, Laney." The moment passed, and then he withdrew his gaze and turned to his father. "Dad, she's not going back to a hotel. Where can we keep her safe?"

Laney opened her mouth to object but shut it just as quickly. They were right. Even she didn't want to risk being alone in a hotel if whoever had planted that bomb came back to finish the job. Besides, she didn't have a suitcase anymore or a means of transportation.

"She can stay with your mother and me." Jim turned

to her. "Mary's always got a guest room at the ready, and she'd love to see you again."

"Thank you, Mr. Mitchell."

His lips quirked. "You can call me Jim, Laney."

Right. She wasn't a kid anymore. Old habits died hard. "Thanks, Jim."

Staying with Ryan's parents might not be ideal, but it beat the other options in town. Like her mother's trailer—the thought made her throat clamp shut. Or even worse, Ryan's place. The case alone would necessitate more time together than she wanted. No reason to compound the awkwardness with evening chats on the deck, if he had one.

But when they reached the Mitchell family home twenty minutes later, Mary hugged both Laney and Ryan tightly and insisted Ryan stay for the night.

"Laney can stay in the guest room, and you can take the sleeper sofa in the basement." She glanced at Laney and shrugged. "I turned his bedroom into my sewing space."

"Mom—"

"Don't argue with me, young man. Your father told me what happened. Someone needs to look after you both."

And then she eyed them in a way that made Laney squirm in her high heels. She could've been sixteen again, coming over for dinner before Ryan took her out to a Friday night game. Like Jim, Mary hadn't changed much. A few more streaks of gray in the dark hair she always wore pulled back in a bun. A bit of extra chubbiness in her soft cheeks. But her mannerisms, her tone, the kindness radiating from her eyes—it was all still there, making Laney feel like she'd fallen into a time warp.

Even their house looked the same, down to the arrangement of the furniture and the pictures on the walls. The family portrait over the mantel made her heart hurt. Jenna was in it, seated beside Ryan—they'd had that picture taken the winter before Jenna vanished. Jim and Mary had left it up all these years.

"Come on," Mary said, squeezing her arm. "It's late. Let's get you settled. We'll pick up some things for you at the store later, if you want to write us a list."

"Tomorrow we'll go to the bog." Ryan's voice cracked, and he cleared his throat.

As she followed Mary, she cast a last glance back at him. For a brief moment, as their gazes locked, something flickered between them—the shared bond of the past, the weight of memories too permanent for time to erase. But then he blinked, and she turned back to walk the familiar path through his house.

Ryan tossed and turned all night. Maybe it was the bruises and the itching ache of the burns on his back, or the trauma of the explosion, or the fact someone had tried to hurt Laney. But more likely, he suspected, it was knowing she was sleeping upstairs in the bedroom that used to be Jenna's. The one where she'd crashed so many nights back in high school when the three of them had stayed out late at a school event or Laney's mom was drunk and Laney couldn't bear the thought of sleeping at home in that squalid trailer.

How often he'd taken for granted his own childhood and how secure it'd been compared to what Laney had endured. No wonder she'd wanted to escape.

But ten years' perspective still couldn't erase the bitter regrets she'd left trailing in her wake, or the sense of abandonment. Maybe he could understand her better now, as an adult, but he'd be a fool to let her close again.

Thankfully, as they leaned against the countertop drinking coffee in silence the next morning, she didn't seem any more interested in reopening the past than he was.

He gestured at her blue jeans and brown T-shirt. Bright red painted toenails peeked out from beneath the cuffs of her too-long pants. "Mom found you some clothes?"

"She ran out to the store early this morning and picked these up, along with some toiletries. It was thoughtful of her." Laney's lips tilted. "She guessed my size, though."

Without her heels, she didn't even reach his shoulder now. An image flashed into his mind of their last dance, that night at senior prom when he'd held her close, her head tucked beneath his chin. But he refrained from making any comment that might veer close to remembering the way things used to be. One thing was for sure, he wasn't letting her out of his sight today. Not with a crime scene to investigate and a potential killer on the loose.

His father strode in through the front door a few minutes later. "You two ready to go?"

Ryan set down his mug and followed Laney to the door, where she pulled on socks and laced up a pair of his mother's old boots. She gave him a wry smile. "Best we could manage under the circumstances."

"I can take you to find a new pair later, if you like." Despite how she'd hurt him, his insides warmed anyway. The interaction felt so…normal, as if they could actually become friends again. *Friends*, not anything more.

His father drove them to Ryan's place, a well-maintained town house in an area of newer construction. Ryan dashed inside to grab a change of clothes before he and Laney took his car to the police station. He'd have to pick up a replacement cruiser while his was in the shop.

"Nice place," Laney said as they pulled out of his complex to head to the station. "I don't recall seeing those before."

"Thanks. They were built after you left." It took a serious effort to keep the bitterness from leaking into his voice at those last two words. A place like his would've been just what Laney wanted back in the old days.

But there were other, more pressing concerns than expired daydreams, like getting Laney over to the bog. They'd had to assign an officer to patrol the crime scene to keep both the press and curious locals from messing with the evidence. But first, they needed to go over the files Hannah had pulled to see if Laney recognized any of the potential bombing suspects.

She followed him through the maze of desks and cabinets to a room at the back. After pulling up an extra chair for Laney, he settled into his seat and logged on to his computer. A few clicks later, he opened the first file, which contained a photograph and personal records on a Delta employee from Indianapolis.

"What are we looking for?" Laney asked as she scooched her chair closer to his. A light fragrance—peaches, maybe—wafted from her. A scent he didn't remember, another reminder that she wasn't the same eighteen-year-old girl anymore. And yet that didn't stop him from wanting to slip an arm around her shoulders and tuck her against his side.

He kept his fingers firmly wrapped around the computer mouse. "We're still working on getting the video footage, so…anyone you recognize. Anything in the file that shows a possible connection with you or the case."

"Okay, I can do that." She leaned closer to the screen, scanning the picture of a middle-aged woman with long blond hair. "I think this is the woman who checked the bag for me in Indianapolis at the gate."

"Did you hand it off to her directly?"

"No, I had to wheel it down the boarding ramp and leave it near the door to the plane. Baggage handlers took it from there."

"So, not likely it was her." He dragged the file into a new folder on his desktop.

Half an hour later, they'd sorted the pile into three stacks—unlikely, possible and unknown potential suspects. It wasn't much of a start, but until they got the security footage, there was little else to be done. He'd pressed her for a description of the man who'd handed her the suitcase at Evansville Regional, but she couldn't positively identify him among the pictures they had.

"Brown hair, hazel eyes. Weathered face." She shrugged apologetically. "I'm sorry. I would've paid better attention if I'd known it was important. You know me, Ryan. I can't even remember what I ate for lunch yesterday." A hint of pink crept across her cheeks at the admission.

It was true. He *did* know her. She had an incredible memory—could ace any test in school—yet forget where she'd parked the car outside the Indianapolis Motor Speedway because the detail didn't seem important at the time. The memory of wandering that scorching parking lot for hours filled his chest with warmth. Back then, he'd been right at her side to help with the things that slipped through the cracks.

Everything had changed…and yet here she was again, needing his help once more.

"That's okay, I get it." He fought to keep a smile off his face and instead pushed his chair back from the desk. "We'll find out who did it. In the meantime, let's get over to the crime scene. The sooner you can examine the remains, the sooner we can get you home to safety."

And if he were being honest, it wasn't only her physical well-being he was concerned about. It was the little problem that this new Laney Hamilton was just as mesmerizing as the old one had been, and every minute he spent with her took him one step closer to saying or doing something stupid. Sending her back to DC as soon as possible was the best course of action for them both.

THREE

Ryan couldn't stop glancing Laney's direction as they headed east out of town toward the bog. In a place as small as Sandy Bluff, with one high school, a Dairy Queen and a shopping center they called a mall only because it had a JCPenney, entertainment had to be invented rather than purchased. The city had grown a bit in the past ten years, but back when he and Laney were in school, they'd spent weekends and long summers traversing the outskirts of town looking for fun and mischief.

Cliff diving at the quarry, despite the no-trespassing signs plastered everywhere.

Late night tag in the farmers' fields.

Throwing biscuits at the cars on the hairpin bend on Fourth Street.

He still hadn't confessed to his parents half the things they'd done. And, as he all too painfully remembered in his quiet times with the Lord, he hadn't been bothered by any Christian morals back then.

How many of those memories were racing through Laney's head right now as she watched the farms and forests roll past? Did she share his sense of extra regret, knowing how they'd been disappointing not only earthly authorities but their heavenly Father as well? Maybe one day he'd muster the courage to ask her, but not now. Not where they were headed.

The air between them felt thick with unspoken thoughts by the time he pulled the squad car onto a dirt road running adjacent to the bog. Bushes, spongy sphagnum moss and wildflowers concealed the muddy bottom, where water pooled up to three feet deep in places. On the far side of the bog, the ground rose to meet dense forest.

He followed the bumpy road a short distance until they reached another patrol car. Pulling in behind it, he shut off the engine and climbed out. The air smelled of humidity and mud and rotting vegetation. A ring of yellow police tape was visible about a hundred feet into the bog, where an officer stood on watch.

Laney followed Ryan to the trunk. He pulled out two sets of hip waders.

"Did you remove any of the remains yet?" she asked, leaning against the car to pull off her shoes and slide her legs into the green fabric and rubber boots. The hip waders practically swallowed her whole.

"Only what the kids turned over to us—the femur and some small bones we think are part of a hand. I imagine you'll need them shipped back to your lab?"

She nodded, but her gaze was distant as if her thoughts were elsewhere.

As he pulled on his waders, another officer climbed out of the other car and Ryan waved him over.

"Cam Peters, this is our bones expert, Laney Hamilton."

She shook his hand. "Nice to meet you, Cam."

"I remember you." Cam smiled, pointing a finger at her. "Sandy Bluff High, class of '11, right? I was a sophomore that year. You and this guy—" he smacked Ryan's arm "—you were thick as thieves, weren't you? What happened?"

Her cheeks flushed, and Ryan shifted his weight. *Awkward.* After Jenna's disappearance and then Laney leaving him, it'd taken months for his name to vanish from the gossip circles. Too bad anyone still remembered.

He cleared his throat. "No one from the press out here today?"

"Not yet," Cam said. "Though once word gets out that we're collecting the bones, I'm sure that will change."

"Well, let's get to it." Ryan pulled some evidence bags from the car along with a collection kit containing gloves, a couple of bristle brushes, tweezers and various other implements.

Each step through the mucky bog produced a gooey, suction-y sort of sound, and gnats and flies buzzed around their faces and necks. When they reached the crime scene, he waved at the other officer and held up the yellow tape to allow Laney to duck underneath. The air hung still for a moment as she waited, watching him.

He tugged at his shirt collar. Cam and the other officers could never understand what these bones might mean to his family, not at a visceral level. But Laney knew, and more importantly, she'd feel it almost as much as he would. Sure, Jenna was his twin sister, but she'd also been Laney's best friend since grade school. Since before he'd finally worked up the nerve to ask Laney to the homecoming dance in ninth grade.

That was half the reason he'd been so shocked when she left town as soon as the prayer vigil ended. His parents' church and their circle of friends had insisted on holding the service to give them a sense of closure once the search was called off. Who were they kidding? There could be no closure for him or his parents. A member of their family had vanished, and they might never know what had happened to her.

Laney couldn't possibly have found closure, either, and yet she'd just…left. Like none of them mattered. He gritted his teeth, ignoring the way his stomach hardened. No reason to prod at the scar tissue over that wound.

Her dark eyes didn't reveal anything now either. Did she expect him to crack and fall apart in front of her and the others?

Not going to happen. No matter what they found.

He pushed ahead, pointing to a muddy gap between a clump of squishy-looking bog plants and a tuft of moss. A single, obvious bone fragment stuck out of the mud. "The kids were able to show us the approximate area where they'd found the bones. After the department's forensics team located and examined the site, the chief made the call to bring in outside help."

Laney knelt on the tuft of moss and held out a hand to take a pair of gloves from Cam. She prodded gently at the exposed piece of bone but didn't move anything. "You've photographed this already?"

Ryan nodded. "We've got a camera with us to record the excavation of the remains."

"Excellent." She glanced up at him, something flickering across her face. "There's no guarantee these bones are from…any of your cold cases." Her voice trailed away, and he knew what she'd wanted to say.

These remains might not be Jenna. We might have to keep living with the uncertainty.

"I know," he said. "But if these bones are human,

they're somebody's cold case. Somebody who deserves to know what happened."

Her jaw tightened as she pressed her lips together. "Then let's get to work."

The only visible bone was splintered, with maybe three inches protruding from the sulfurous-smelling muck. If she had to guess from the diameter, Laney would say it was a fibula, the smaller bone of the lower leg. But she'd have to remove it to know.

"The damage here looks recent," she said, pointing at the tip of the bone and glancing up at Ryan. "See how the edge along this break is colored differently? It hasn't been exposed to water as long."

He nodded. "Maybe the teenagers broke it?"

"Or an animal. Or whatever brought these remains closer to the surface." Partly it depended on how long and how deeply they'd been buried, but she didn't want to speculate. Not with how important these bones could be.

She pulled a trowel out of the kit Cam had placed next to her and gently scooped mud away from the bone, one thin layer at a time. Water collected in the space as she cleared it, making for difficult working conditions but better preservation.

The work was slow and painstaking, like an archaeological excavation. Each layer had to be photographed and documented, each bone fragment tagged and placed in a separate bag for later analysis. But the work kept both her hands and mind occupied, leaving little space to reflect on who these bones once belonged to, or the look on Ryan's face as each piece came up out of the ground.

The pile of plastic bags beside her grew steadily larger, but they still hadn't found the skull. Her heart sank a little more with each bone she examined. The signs were all there, but her scientific mind refused to entertain any possibilities yet.

Across the bog, cars had collected on the side of the county highway, and a few of the braver news trucks had pulled onto the dirt road behind the squad cars.

Laney dragged the back of her arm across her forehead, wiping away the growing perspiration. She stood thigh deep in the mud, and while the rubber hip waders kept her legs dry, her arms and shirt were coated in thick muck. Now that it was afternoon, the sun scorched down on their heads, making her wish she'd worn her hat on the plane instead of packing it in her carry-on.

"Here." Ryan passed her a bottle of water. "Do you want to take a break?"

She glanced at the waiting reporters. Sandy Bluff only had one newspaper, and no TV news station. They must've driven in from Evansville and Bloomington. "And face that crowd? No thanks." After a long drink, she recapped the bottle and wedged it into the moss.

"They'll wait us out, you know."

"I know. We have reporters in DC too." She turned back to the excavation. This patch had almost been cleared, but depending on how long the bones had been here, they might find more among the roots of the surrounding plants. "I think it's time to expand our search radius. See what you can find on the other side of these plants."

Ryan traipsed around the back of a clump of swamp milkweed and prodded gingerly at the ground a few feet away.

"So…" He hesitated, and she could feel his question

hanging in the air before the words came out. "What can you tell so far?"

"I try to avoid any conclusions until the bones are clean," she said lightly.

When his brown gaze met hers, the veiled anguish in his eyes nearly stole her breath. "Laney…"

She glanced at the other officers. Cam was occupied snapping photos. The other one had returned to the dirt road to deal with the reporters. Ryan deserved to hear first.

"From what we've unearthed, I'd say female. Approximately five foot six." *Jenna's height.* From the way his eyes shuttered, he had the same thought. "Based on the growth plate on the fibula, I'd guess she was near full height. Late teens."

She hated the way his expression went slack. To have to be the one to deliver this news.

"And—" he cleared his throat "—how long have the remains been here?"

Laney sighed. "It's hard to say. Given the discoloration and cracks forming in the bone, anywhere from eight to twelve years. She's not a recent disappearance."

He pressed a mud-speckled wrist to his mouth and stared beyond her as if he were looking back into the past.

When she tried to speak, it was around a hard lump in her throat. "We need the skull, Ryan. There's a forensic odontologist at the Smithsonian who can compare dental records. For any of your missing persons."

"Right." He turned back to the muck in front of him without meeting her gaze.

Jenna had been like a sister to her, too, but she knew it wasn't the same. She'd walked away from Sandy Bluff, successfully escaping into a brand-new life, but Ryan had

had to live every day here without Jenna for the last decade. Her heart ached for him, but she could hardly say anything in front of the other officers. Instead, she settled for resting one mud-crusted hand lightly on his forearm and squeezed gently. He glanced back at her, shooting her a weak smile before crouching down again to work.

Another half hour of digging in silence yielded two scapulas and a broken clavicle. They were getting close. Laney's fingertips brushed against something round and hard. Big enough to be what they needed. "I've got something," she said. Ryan clambered out of the mud and worked his way back to her as she loosened the sediment around the bone.

Cam hurried to them—a sure sign to the reporters they'd found something critical. They'd have an ordeal getting out of here once they were done.

The camera clicked rapidly as she hunched over, arms beneath the mud and water up to her elbows, fighting to free the object without damaging it. With a last bit of gentle pressure, the bone came loose, and she swirled it slowly in the water as she floated it to the surface.

Any last vestige of hope washed away with the debris as she lifted the skull out of the water. Somewhere in the back of her mind, despite all reason, she'd thought maybe the skull would prove it wasn't Jenna. That there'd be some obvious feature that couldn't possibly have belonged to her.

What she'd told Ryan was true—they couldn't know for sure until the forensic odontologist studied the teeth. But as she rotated the skull in her hands, she could feel the truth deep in her own bones.

Ryan's sharp inhalation of breath pulled her back into the moment. He pointed to an indentation on the back, where the bone had cracked. "A blow to the head?" The words were faint, and he clenched and unclenched one hand as he spoke.

"Yes. And it happened close to the time of death. See these jagged edges? They would've smoothed out if the bone had had time to heal."

He nodded. "I remember from the Wilson trial. The prosecutor pointed out places where the bones had started to remodel."

Laney raised an eyebrow. "He kept his victims alive for a while?"

"Yeah. It was…ugly." His Adam's apple bobbed. "But did that happen in this case? Was this head injury the cause of death?"

"Possibly. It looks more like a homicide than a hit-and-run to me." Her heart twisted as she imagined what could have been Jenna's final moments. "But I need to examine all the bones to say more conclusively."

"All right." He jerked his head toward Cam, who held out a large collection bag for Laney.

She slid the skull inside and attached the identification number. In the distance, the other officer approached from the patrol cars, carrying a large plastic bin. It took another hour to gather the remaining fragments of the skeleton and do one last sweep of the area, but finally all the bones were labeled and secured in the bin.

"Here's the plan." Ryan kept glancing over to the dirt road, where his vehicle was walled in by news trucks and people. "We'll walk directly to the car. I'll escort you around to the passenger side, and you get in. Whatever they ask you, you can tell them it's classified. And do not, under any circumstances, give them your name."

"I grew up in this town. Half those people have probably recognized me already."

"But the less publicity you get, the better." His lips tilted to one side. "Besides, you have mud all over your face."

"Yours isn't much better."

Cam and the other officer hauled the bin of evidence, and she and Ryan followed behind, Ryan shadowing her every step. While she appreciated his concern, that'd be sure to get the rumor mill up and running again for anyone who did recognize her.

The reporters swarmed as they approached, holding out mobile devices and barking questions.

"What did you find in the bog?"

"Are those the remains of college student Madison Smith?"

"What can you tell us about the disappearances? Was Ronald Wilson responsible?"

Laney kept her head low, letting Ryan answer. The same thing over and over, "I'm sorry, the details are classified until we know more."

She'd been around the media plenty of times in DC, but most often at press conferences or post-trial interviews. They didn't usually swarm crime scenes.

Of course, this story was a big deal for Sandy Bluff. From what Ryan had said, more people than his family waited for leads on their missing loved ones. Maybe the reporters had already sniffed out the possibility the real killer was still at large.

She couldn't shake the feeling of claustrophobia as Ryan held the reporters back while she yanked off her muddy hip waders and stuffed them into the trunk. When she'd accepted this job, she'd done it for the Mitchells.

But what had she gotten into? Something that went far deeper than a single cold case. The smart thing to do would be to get these bones packed up and shipped back to the Smithsonian, then book herself the next flight out.

Ryan pried the car door open and she slid into the vehicle, grateful for the metal and glass separating her from the people who wanted answers. By the time he joined her, the two officers had loaded the bin of bones into the other patrol car.

As Laney settled back into her seat, trying to roll the tension out of her shoulders, her cell phone chirped out its cheerful ringtone. She dug for it in her purse, pulse quickening as she stared at the number a second before answering.

"Mom?" She frowned. Her mother *never* called outside their arranged semi-annual chats.

"Laney…" Her voice was so weak, she was barely audible. Laney tapped the button for speaker, and Ryan leaned in closer, straining to hear. "I need help. Now."

"Where are you?" Laney asked, one hand clutching the door handle. Some internal warning pulsed through her system, especially with the way Ryan had tensed beside her. It wouldn't be the first time her mother had overdosed herself or gotten into trouble, but…she had local friends to call. Never Laney.

"Home," her mother rasped. "They've got—"

The line went dead.

FOUR

Ryan took one glance at Laney's blanched face and flipped on his lights and siren, despite the bad timing. The other car could get the evidence back to headquarters without him, and he and Laney could be at her mother's trailer within minutes.

He tilted his face to his shoulder mic and notified the dispatcher, then turned to Laney. "What's her lot number?"

"Thirty-five," Laney supplied, her voice faint. Her knuckles had turned white where she still clung to the door handle.

"You okay?"

She nodded, saying nothing more as the crowd parted before them like the Red Sea. He turned onto the main road heading back toward town, but then turned north again a mile later, taking a road that would lead them to the trailer park. A couple of cars pulled off to the side as he approached.

"I haven't seen her in ten years," Laney murmured.

Of course she'd be worried about her mother. Even though Ryan had never felt anything more than anger toward Kim Hamilton and her destructive life choices, it was only natural Laney would be concerned. And while he suspected this call was some ploy of Kim's to get Laney back into her life, now probably wasn't the time to point that out to Laney.

Now would be the right time to be supportive. Show they could still be friends.

Besides, there was another possibility dancing around in the back of his mind. What if someone was trying to get to Laney through her mother?

She kept talking, letting go of the door to rub her hands back and forth across her denim-clad knees. "I only talk to her twice a year."

He gritted his teeth, despite his best intentions. "You have a good reason for that, Laney." So many times he'd wanted to rescue Laney from her life in that dive of a home. Or demand his father arrest Kim. But the evidence was never enough to press charges, and if it had been, Laney would've ended up in foster care.

They'd gone over their plan so many times. Four years of college at Indiana University for Laney to earn her nursing degree so she could get a job as an RN. He only needed two years at the community college in Evansville before entering the police academy, and then he'd join the force, working for his dad. They'd get married and she'd be able to go back to school for a master's degree if she wanted. Maybe even be a nurse practitioner one day.

Maybe it had been foolish to think it could've worked. At least Laney had escaped, and she'd clearly done well for herself without his help.

The sign for the trailer park loomed in front of them, and he spoke into his shoulder mic, updating the dispatcher on his arrival.

Laney's knees bounced up and down like a pair of

jackhammers. "Please, God. Please let her be okay." The words were muttered under her breath, so low he almost didn't catch them.

Had she found new hope in Christ too? And the means to forgive her mother?

Ryan pulled the car to a stop a trailer down from lot number thirty-five. He rested a hand on Laney's vibrating knee and she glanced at him, startled out of her reverie. "He'll never leave us or forsake us, Laney. Trust His goodness."

Her mouth dropped open, but she clamped it shut, nodding in agreement.

The exterior of the trailer appeared more or less secure, despite its obvious need for repairs. Most of the screens had been torn or were missing from the windows, but nothing sat open. Still, it was better to be safe than sorry, especially after what had happened to Laney at the airport.

He pulled out his gun and reached for the car door handle. "I need you to stay in the car while I check things out. If anything happens, get down and out of sight. Got it?"

Taking her silence for assent, he stepped out of the car. Dust rose from the packed dirt as he walked past the nearest trailer toward Kim's. This place had probably been nice once…fifty years ago. Now it housed the poorest residents of Sandy Bluff, the down-and-out, the suffering and the oppressed. A baby cried inside the thin walls, and his heart broke for the child.

But he wasn't here to bemoan the fate of the residents, he was here to ensure their safety. Stopping on the lower step leading up to the trailer, he rapped on the metal door. "Ms. Hamilton? Can you open the door?"

Silence from inside. He knocked again, harder this time.

"Ms. Hamilton, this is Sergeant Ryan Mitchell. I'm here with Laney. Can you open the door?"

Still no response. Had she passed out? He tried the doorknob. Unlocked. He pushed the door open a couple of inches and called again for Kim, then gritted his teeth when there was no answer. Most likely explanation was that she'd overdosed and required medical attention. The alternative—that somebody was using her to get to Laney—was far more disturbing, especially since Laney had barely had any contact with Kim in a decade. Somebody would have to be pretty familiar with both of them to know the connection.

He glanced back at Laney, still waiting in the car, and then gestured at the door to show he was going in.

He'll never leave us or forsake us, Laney.

Ryan's words replayed through Laney's mind as she watched Ryan push his way into her mother's trailer. He'd found faith in Jesus, too, during the last ten years. After all those times they'd turned down Jenna's invitations to youth group... She must be smiling up in heaven. Laney's heart warmed, thankful for what God had done in his life, but it couldn't change things between them.

Walking away from him all those years ago had been brutal, but she'd had to do it. Had to get away from their mistakes, from what had happened to Jenna. From that night just before graduation when Laney and Ryan had fully given in to their feelings and she'd come *this* close to going full circle and walking her mother's path right back to this trailer park.

She picked absently at the fabric of the patrol car's seat. Hard to believe she'd grown up here, riding her bicycle barefoot around these packed dirt roads. The place looked even more squalid than she remembered. Her mother's trailer would never have graced the cover of *Country Living* magazine, but it had decayed even further in the past ten years. Dents in the side, rust along the windows, one screen hanging off at a weird angle.

An image flashed into her mind of the day she'd left. Her mother had stared out the window, her shoulders slumped and her mousy brown hair hanging limp against pale cheeks, as Laney explained she'd be going to Jenna Mitchell's vigil and then catching a ride to the nearest Greyhound station to head out of town.

Permanently.

She had a single duffel of clothing packed—she'd had it packed for weeks—and the strap had dug into her shoulder as she'd stood with one hand on the door. Waiting for anything, any reason to stay.

Her mother hadn't turned, not even when Laney had slammed that stupid aluminum screen door shut. Laney had said her goodbyes to the Mitchells and, with her university acceptance in hand, escaped to build a better life.

Only now she was back.

Black flashed at the corner of her eye, startling her out of the memory. Instinctively she pulled away from the passenger-side window as something smashed into it. She screamed as it shattered, covering the floor and the seat and her lap with cascading fragments of safety glass.

She fumbled for her seat belt, fingers connecting with the button. A dark figure loomed outside the window, and a gloved hand shot inside, fingers grasping for the shoulder of her T-shirt.

Laney's heart catapulted into her throat. She swiveled in the seat out of reach, throwing her feet against the inside of the passenger door. Kicking hard, she launched herself backward over the center console, her spine dragging painfully over Ryan's equipment.

Her attacker groped inside the car, catching the oversize boot on Laney's left foot and yanking her back toward the door. Laney's throat burned from screaming, and she struck with her free foot at the knife looming perilously close to her leg.

The boot came free and she pulled both legs back into the relative safety of the driver's seat. Her fingers scrabbled for the driver's-side door latch and she pulled, falling backward out the door. Footsteps pounded on the hard earth as her attacker ran around the back of the car. Laney dove behind the open door and crawled on all fours to the front, searching the ground for anything she could use to defend herself.

In the distance, a door banged open. *Ryan?* Footfalls thumped at the far end of the car, and Laney glanced around the bumper to see a black figure dashing toward the gap between the nearest two trailers.

"Freeze!" Ryan commanded, his voice filling her chest with relief. He stood on the steps outside the trailer, gun out and aiming at the back of the squad car.

But her attacker ignored the order and dove behind the nearest trailer, out of sight. Without hesitating, Ryan leaped off the steps and sprinted past Laney in hot pursuit.

Her heart beat double time, but she swallowed in a couple of deep breaths and climbed back into the police car. It took a few tries to find the right button to activate the radio in the center console. She had no idea what codes Ryan would have used, but when the dispatcher answered, she sputtered out an account of what had happened. The dispatcher told her backup would arrive within ten minutes. She sat behind the wheel, waiting in eerie silence for the report of a gunshot or some other telltale sign Ryan had caught up with her attacker.

God, please keep him safe.

An engine roared to life on the far side of the trailer park. Was it some unsuspecting resident or the getaway car?

She tapped her fingers on the steering wheel for a few eternal minutes before Ryan jogged back into view, face red from exertion and gun secured back in its holster. His eyes widened briefly as he scanned the road for her, until she waved from inside the car.

A moment later, he knelt beside the open driver's-side door, his face lined with concern. "Laney, are you all right?"

She gave herself a quick once-over, looking for any sign of injury. Everything felt normal, though she still bore fragments of safety glass on her clothing. "Yeah, I think I'm okay." She glanced at Ryan, her lips twisting. "I *tried* to wait in the car like you said."

He raised an eyebrow, humor wrestling with the worry in his dark eyes. "You never were any good at following instructions."

Laney hid a smile. "I take it whoever it was got away?"

"Unfortunately, yes. He had a truck waiting a few streets over. With that ski mask he was wearing, I didn't get a good visual. Give me a minute and I'll call it in."

"Already done," she said as she climbed out of the car. "Backup will be here any minute."

Ryan quirked an eyebrow. "Nice work. Then I'll report the getaway car."

She stood to one side, brushing glass fragments and dirt off her clothes as Ryan's voice drifted from the inside of the police cruiser. *"Blue Ford truck, pre-1997..."*

He returned a moment later. "They'll dispatch somebody to look for the truck. Henderson and Johnson will be here in five to help gather evidence."

Another crime scene. How many more would she be part of before this case ended? Or someone ended *her*?

And the million-dollar question behind it all—why? Why her, when dozens of other forensic anthropologists could take her place?

She shivered, then glanced back at her mother's trailer. "Is Mom okay?"

Ryan frowned. "You screamed before I found her. But given what just happened, I'd say this was a setup."

"Mom would never—"

"Not willingly," he said grimly.

Her breath froze in her lungs, and she started for the trailer, but Ryan caught her hand, pulling her to a stop. Electricity buzzed up her arm, even though he let go almost as soon as his fingers wrapped around hers. "Let me go first, okay? The coast is probably clear now, but just to be safe."

She nodded, furling and unfurling the hand he'd touched as she followed him up to the trailer's front door. When was the last time he'd held her hand like that? It had been a long time, long enough that her insides shouldn't be this warm. But there was no denying the security she felt standing next to him or how glad she was not to face this moment alone.

The cheap screen door was long gone, leaving only rusty hinges behind. He stepped up into the trailer, gun at the ready, and motioned to Laney to wait. On the far side of him, a fluorescent light flickered over the sink of the narrow galley kitchen. Nothing moved.

He passed out of her view, his steps echoing back to

her off the indoor-outdoor carpet that had been too thin back when Laney still walked on it every day. The only way things had ever been repaired or replaced was if Laney did it herself. She still marveled at the fact that her mother had held down her job at the local discount store for this long.

The waiting felt like an eternity, each second ticking by so slowly Ryan must've surely searched the entire trailer by now. From somewhere inside, his radio crackled to life, and his voice carried through the thin walls, speaking in acronyms and police code Laney couldn't understand. But there was no mistaking the urgency in his voice.

She launched herself up the steps and into the entry without waiting for permission. Familiar smells assaulted her nostrils—ramen noodles and rotting trash, polyester upholstery, and the faintest scent of marijuana, mostly covered up by her mother's favorite, cheap vanilla-spice candles. She could be seventeen again, still trapped in this unbearable life with no way out. Her knees went momentarily weak.

No, this isn't who I am. God, You pulled me out of this wreck. She forced her feet to move, weaving through the narrow hallway past the kitchen and into the living room. A single lamp in the corner bathed the room in sickly yellow light.

She froze in the doorway.

Her mother was tied to a hard kitchen chair, her mouth gagged, head lolling to one side. Ryan knelt in front of her, cutting loose the ropes that held her to the chair. But the blood…so much blood.

It pooled around her feet and beneath her hands, dripping from both arms as they dangled at her sides. Angry red gashes sliced across white skin on both wrists.

Laney couldn't stop staring, her pulse roaring in her ears. Her mother certainly wasn't always mentally stable, but she hadn't done this to herself. "Is she...gone?"

"Laney, you shouldn't be—" He turned, took one look at her face and pressed his lips together. "She's still alive but losing blood fast. We need to get pressure on the cuts. Grab some towels?"

She crossed the space to the kitchen and yanked two dish towels out of the drawer—exactly where her mother kept them years ago—then dashed back out to the living room to help Ryan ease Kim off the chair and onto the floor. She was frailer than Laney remembered, her hair more gray than brown, her wan face etched with deep wrinkles. Too worn for someone who was only in her midforties.

Laney caught up one of the wrists, pressing the towel tightly against the wound to try to stem the flow. She glanced at Ryan as he did the same, but he wasn't looking at her. His gaze had settled on the wall beyond her, where a narrow window looked out on the front when the curtains weren't closed.

To the right of the window, something had been scrawled, obscured by the semidarkness. She squinted at the words, made harder to read by the fact that they appeared to be dripping down the wall.

"Laney..." Ryan's tone sent a little shiver running down her spine.

Was that...blood? Her stomach curdled.

Ryan dug a flashlight out of his utility belt and flipped it on. The words popped into sharp clarity.

I see you.

FIVE

Laney paced back and forth in the waiting area, her thoughts running in a million different directions. Her mother had been taken into a room immediately after the ambulance arrived at the ER, and two hours later, they still hadn't heard anything. The delay was almost more than she could stand.

As were Ryan's attempts to get her to leave town before she'd even done a preliminary assessment of the remains. He sat in one of the waiting room chairs, one foot propped up across his other knee, occasionally running a muscular hand through his dark hair.

"Look, Laney, this case has exploded beyond what any of us anticipated. What just happened with your mother—that was a setup to get to you. You, specifically. Somebody is after you, somebody who knows who your mother is and where she lives. This isn't just about the remains anymore and what we might uncover. We need to book your flight now, and we'll get those bones packed up first thing in the morning." He dug his phone out of his back pocket and tapped at the screen.

"Hold on." She sank into the seat next to him, reaching to grab his wrist but stopping just shy of touching him.

No reason to go there. "I'm not bailing that fast. We don't even know how Mom is doing yet. And what about the investigation on the bomb? Don't you need me to watch the security footage?"

"I need you not to get hurt."

Something about the warmth in his tone and the way his eyes softened triggered warning bells. But surely he didn't *still* have feelings for her after what she'd done. "Ryan…"

He waved a hand impatiently. "This isn't about you and me. I'd say the same thing to anyone we brought in on a case. The reason you flew out here was to help recover the remains. There's no reason to put you in any more danger now that we've got the bones."

Of course his words made sense. That disappointment pricking at her insides related to the case, not to how easily he'd brushed her aside. She popped back up to her feet, nodding far more vigorously than necessary.

"Good, I'm glad we have that cleared up. You should know the Smithsonian has given me clearance to stay as long as necessary, so I'll be the one making the call about when I go. And I'm not leaving without taking a preliminary look at those bones, especially after what happened with my suitcase. What if somebody finds a way to blow up the UPS truck?"

His lips pressed together. "I'm glad to see ten years hasn't made a dent in your determination to have your own way."

Was he teasing her or lashing out? Did he truly think she was so petty, that she'd left him all those years ago solely to get her way? It was too late to find out now. She wasn't going to reopen that can of worms. Far better to keep things casual. Distant.

She shrugged. "When life throws obstacles in your path, you have to find a way to get around them."

Hurt flickered in his eyes, but she turned away. She'd loved him once with every fiber of her teenage being, so much she'd almost lost sight of what mattered most—escaping Sandy Bluff before she became permanently entangled. When the wake-up call had come, she'd taken it. Now wasn't the time to second-guess that decision.

The doctor's arrival spared her more awkward conversation. His face was unreadable as he stood in the doorway, one hand holding a tablet, the other tucked into his white coat.

Ryan stood, asking the question at the same time she did. "How is she?"

"She's in stable condition. We repaired the damaged blood vessels, and she's starting her second unit of blood. In a couple of hours, she'll be moved to the medical-surgical unit for observation, but you're welcome to come look in on her now. We'll need to keep her here for a couple of nights."

Some of the tension eased in Laney's chest. Sure, she and her mom had never been close, but she felt terrible knowing someone had hurt Kim because of her involvement in this case.

"You should know something else," the doctor said, lowering his voice. "We found methamphetamine in her system, along with traces of other illegal narcotics. If she's addicted, now might be a good time to consider a rehab program."

Laney gave Ryan a sidelong glance, but he hardly looked surprised. As they followed the doctor back to her mother's room, he confided, "Officers will have to search the trailer. It's a crime scene."

"I know."

"I wish they'd had a reason to do it fifteen years ago," he muttered.

Then I would've been a foster kid on top of everything else. She bit the inside of her cheek instead of saying it out loud. Her mother had been seventeen when Laney was born, and Kim's string of poor choices had followed Laney like a mangy dog. Ryan meant well—he always had—but the only way to escape the shame of her upbringing and the mistakes of the past was the way she had done it.

Leave, and never look back.

Her mother was asleep, eyes closed, arms resting on top of a hospital blanket. An IV drip holding a bag of blood was hooked into one arm, and both wrists were bandaged. In the background, the monitoring machines blinked with each steady beat of her heart.

Laney reached for the nearest hand, wrapping her fingers around her mother's thin, cold ones. Forty-five, and she looked twenty years older. She'd made life harder with her choices, but for the first time, Laney couldn't help feeling compassion for her. And the tiniest bit of respect, that her mother had not only seen the pregnancy through to birth but kept Laney with no outside support or help.

Her throat clamped. Seventeen was far too young to have that kind of responsibility.

Ryan's warm hand on her shoulder pulled her out of her thoughts. "Can I pray for her?" he whispered.

She nodded, blinking away the moisture forming in her eyes. If only her teenage father had been a man like Ryan, instead of a lowlife who'd pretended she never happened. "I'd like that."

* * *

Stars filled the dark summer sky by the time Ryan escorted Laney out of the hospital. She'd been through a crushing twenty-four hours, and yet she remained as calm and determined as ever.

"Are we heading back to the station?" she asked as they walked through the parking lot toward his car.

He quirked a brow. "It's nearly eleven o'clock at night. Aren't you tired? Or starving? *I'm* starving." His stomach growled as if to punctuate his words. Besides, even though they'd washed up at the hospital, they'd spent half the day in a bog.

From the set of her jaw as he unlocked the car, food wasn't a high priority. "I want to start my preliminary exam on the bones."

"I get that, but it's been a long couple of days. You might miss something if you're running on empty." He opened the door for her before getting in on his side. "And my back is killing me." The burn wounds had been dressed and well covered, but a whole day of work plus chasing that suspect had been harder on his body than he wanted to admit.

"All right." She let out a little sigh, lifting dark strands of hair on her cheek. "I'm a bit battered myself."

He turned on the ignition and pulled the car out of the garage, then headed down the main road. Sandy Bluff wasn't exactly known for its night life, but there was a Steak 'n Shake that stayed open this late. A few intersections later, the red sign over a black-and-white awning glowed off to the right with its promise of shoestring fries, fresh burgers and milkshakes.

"No way. This place is still here?" Laney asked as he pulled into the lot.

He arched an eyebrow. "Some things never change."

Maybe it was risky taking her back to one of their old haunts, but there wasn't anywhere else to get a meal at this hour.

She climbed out of the car, a tiny smile tickling her lips. "Are we hitting Dairy Queen next?"

He forced his gaze away from her mouth. "You can only hope." Flirting… Why was he flirting with Laney Hamilton again? No matter how good it felt, it was a bad idea.

He had every intention of holding the front door for her, like a gentleman, but she beat him to the handle. Probably her own way of declaring boundaries.

She stopped so abruptly on the black mat inside the door that he nearly ran into her. "This place hasn't changed at all."

"Our…" He paused. Maybe it was a stupid thing to say, but he couldn't help it. "Our booth is still there." The long one in the corner, where they'd sat with Jenna and Ryan's best friend Ben. Sometimes a handful of other kids, depending on the night.

Sometimes just the two of them, sharing a shake and fighting over the last of the fries. Ten years, and the memories were as fresh as if it'd been yesterday. Did Laney feel it too?

"Look at that," she said, shaking her head.

He extended a hand, determined to put the ball in her court. "Pick us a table."

His heart sank just a little—foolish as it was—when she chose a table near the window at the opposite end of the dining room. As if she wanted to get as far away from the memories as she could.

Laney propped open her menu, though he suspected

she still had the whole thing memorized. She'd been able to recite every item verbatim, with the price, back when they were in high school. Always on a dare. Those little green hot peppers in the bottle on the table had a wicked burn, as he'd learned by losing to her more than a few times.

The waitress trotted over, and something danced in Laney's eyes as she glanced at him over the top of her menu. "I'll have the double Steakburger, fries and a cookies 'n cream shake."

"And I'll have the same." A grin was trying to break out on his lips, and he gave in. "I thought you might have grown out of burgers and ordered a salad."

"Ha, never. Well, not at a restaurant anyway. I can make a salad at home." She sobered and gazed at the empty tables. "Do you ever see anybody from high school?"

"Stephanie married some old guy, a doctor, and moved away. Brittany and Todd stayed together through college, but he left her. She still lives in town with her parents and her daughter."

Laney held up a hand to stop him. "Forget I asked. Coming back here is like being on the set of *Dr. Phil.*"

"It's not *all* bad." He paused as the waitress delivered steaming plates of food, along with tall, frosty milkshakes. "I still get together with Ben once in a while. And the guys on the force, they're pretty great."

She squirted ketchup onto her plate, then took her time dragging a clump of skinny shoestring fries through the red sauce. "Did you end up going to the community college? Or did you go to one of the big schools?"

He'd come *this* close to applying to Indiana University the year after she left. The thought that she might be only a few hours away, walking around campus, taking classes, dating other men...

But in the end, he couldn't do it. "I couldn't leave Mom and Dad. Not with everything that happened. Two years of classes were enough to qualify for the police academy, and then I joined the force afterward." He took a bite of burger, chewing in silence for a moment. Laney kept her eyes on her plate, as if she knew they were treading into territory she wanted to avoid. But they could hardly eat a meal together without catching up on *some* level. Finally he said, "It's clear you've done well for yourself. Dad said you ended up at West Carolina?"

"Yeah, for undergrad. I transferred after a year at IU. Their forensics program is excellent. Then I did an MA and PhD at Boston University. The Smithsonian hired me as a postdoctoral fellow a couple years ago."

"So, what you're saying is you're too smart to hang out with someone like me?"

Her mouth hung open for a moment, until he winked.

"Just messing with you." When her cheeks tinged pink, he added, "But I am proud of you, Laney. I hope you know I've always been behind you, one hundred percent. Regardless of what happened between us."

He rubbed a hand against the back of his neck, suddenly aware of how uncomfortable he might be making their working relationship by spewing every thought that popped into his head. Because a lot *had* happened between them, and some of those things he'd take back in a heartbeat—like that June night before graduation. But it was too late to live in past regrets now, and apologizing would only make things worse.

"Thanks," she mumbled and took a sip of her milkshake.

An awkward moment passed in which he could've cut the silence with a knife, until he thought of another question he'd wanted to ask. "Why'd you give up on nursing and switch to forensics?" Laney had always been top-notch at science, so it wasn't a stretch, but she'd also always wanted to help people.

She grew thoughtful for a moment. "After Jenna disappeared and I learned firsthand what it was like to go through a loss like that…I wanted a different way to help, I guess. To give other families answers, even if we couldn't get them for ourselves."

He stirred the dregs of his milkshake with his straw. "Did you think maybe one day you'd be able to help us too?"

"With remains?" Her lips tilted down into a half frown. "That possibility has always been there, but honestly, I never really thought we'd find her. Not after all this time. We still might not have." After a pause, she cleared her throat. "So, the case… Tell me about the homicide and the man you convicted. What kind of possible connections are we looking for?"

Relief took the edge off his nerves. Dealing with junk from the past was hard, but the case brought him back to solid ground. Facts and evidence and reports and data.

"His name's Ronald Wilson, fifty-seven years old, convicted of murdering a twenty-year-old woman two years ago. The body was found in the dumpster behind the gas station where she worked, though she'd been missing for several weeks before she was found. Evidence suggested she was killed elsewhere, dismembered and then dumped. His hair was found on the body." He paused. "You sure you want to hear about this while you're eating?"

Laney shrugged, taking another pull on her shake. "I'm a forensic anthropologist. I'm used to it. Go on."

"You always had a stomach of steel." Like that time he'd come down with the stomach flu on their way home from a field trip to the state capitol building... Laney had calmly rubbed his back while he heaved into his empty lunch box, even though everyone around them was rushing to crack open the bus windows. She'd always been there for him back in those days. "Anyway, when we searched his home, we found the murder weapon buried in the backyard."

"Which was...?"

"A crowbar."

This was why he was a police officer—to protect as many people as he could from the ones who attacked others with crowbars.

He continued, "We also found the knife used on the body sitting in a knife block in his kitchen and a marked map in one of his desk drawers. The map led us to two sets of remains—girls who'd been killed a few years earlier."

"Interesting. Why would he hold on to a map like that? Or mark it in the first place?" She grimaced. "And why on earth would he use one of his kitchen knives?"

Ryan shrugged. "That's the creepy thing about serial killers. They like trophies. Souvenirs to mark their kills. When we unearthed the other bodies, we found the same cut marks on all three sets of remains. Same blade."

"Strange. Why would he bury two of the victims but dump the third in such a public place?"

"I asked myself the same thing," he answered, pointing a fry at her as he talked. "Wilson pleaded innocent during the trial—insisted he was framed—but the prosecution had an ironclad case against him and no other suspects. With nothing else to go on, we had to let it go."

"What do *you* think?"

"At the time, I was happy drop it, especially since we knew he couldn't have been responsible for Jenna. But now, with this new disappearance and the fact that someone is after you... I'm not so sure."

"You've got both the knife blade and the records?"

He nodded.

"Good. I'll compare them with the bones we found today and look to see whether or not we can attribute the death to Wilson." She pushed her plate aside.

The waitress dropped off their tabs, and he snatched Laney's up before she could get to it. "This one's on me. Because you're helping us out by being here."

She frowned but didn't object. "I guess that's a decent-enough reason."

After paying, they walked back to the car. Laney had grown silent again, which for her, usually meant only one thing—those gears in her mind were hard at work, cranking through who knew how many possibilities and ideas.

After they'd gotten in the car and started for his parents' house, she finally voiced her thoughts. "If we find proof Wilson was framed and you all arrested the wrong man... That means the person who's after me is a serial killer."

"Hey." He placed a hand on hers, squeezing gently. "I'm going to keep you safe until we can get you out of here."

And the sooner that happened, the better. Both for Laney's safety *and* the sake of his own heart.

SIX

The next morning, Laney sat hunched over a microscope in the tiny dedicated lab space of the Sandy Bluff police station. She'd already spent an hour on the phone arranging for a social worker to get her mother into rehab. The security footage from both airports had come in overnight, too, and as soon as she finished the preliminary examination of yesterday's remains, they'd have several hours' worth of video to watch.

So long as Ryan gave up trying to rush her home. Of course she understood why—not only because of the potential killer after her but also because being around each other again was growing increasingly uncomfortable. How long could she keep putting off an apology? And if she apologized for leaving him so abruptly, then what? Friendship? DMs and phone calls? A long-distance relationship?

What would she even *want* to come next?

Nothing. The question was dangerous, and she needed to put it out of her mind. That chapter of her life was over, and it was better not to let Ryan back in at all. Ties to this dead-end town were too risky to her mental health. No matter how natural it felt being around him again.

Thankfully, he'd left her to examine the bones in peace, though it wouldn't be long before he wanted an update. The tools they had available paled in comparison to her lab at the Smithsonian, but she could still make a number of preliminary observations.

A clipboard lay on the counter beside her, containing a stack of papers to document her findings. Each bone had to be removed one at a time, its identification number and pertinent data recorded, and key evidence documented by both drawings and photographs, which would then be uploaded onto the computer. She could spend weeks going over these in her lab. Here, she didn't have the luxury of time.

Instead, she selectively examined the bones that had caught her eye during the excavation. The ones with broken or cut ends and the ones she knew from experience were most likely to be damaged by a killer.

The thought of finding the evidence that would lock the murderer away behind bars was what made the whole nightmare bearable. Each cut represented an unthinkable act of violence against another human being, and her heart would be an aching mass of grief if it weren't for the ability she'd honed to distance herself from the reality of what had happened to the victim. Especially if she stopped long enough to consider who this particular victim might've been.

And Ryan—how was he going to take whatever they found? She'd emailed photographs of the teeth and skull to her team's forensic odontologist first thing that morning, along with dental records for Jenna and another missing girl who'd vanished a year after her. He'd need the actual skull to make a conclusive statement, but the photographs would provide enough to get a soft decision.

Was there any result that would be good?

"Hey, how's it going?" Ryan popped his head through the door much sooner than she felt prepared for.

She swallowed. "Okay. I've found and documented evidence of cut marks on several of the bones. Once you pull the files on Ronald Wilson, we'll be able to compare the cuts to determine similarities between his victims and this one. If you can get the actual bones from his victims to my lab at the Smithsonian, we can make a more detailed comparison. Angle of the blade, amount of pressure applied, which hand the killer favored. Things like that."

"And the things you told me yesterday, at the bog? You still think you have the time of death correct?"

"Within a couple of years."

Her cell phone vibrated, and she pulled off her nitrile gloves to dig it out of her pocket. A text from the Smithsonian.

A lump formed in her throat, and she coughed to clear it as she unlocked the screen and pulled up the text.

She'd known this could happen—felt in her bones that it *would*—but still nothing had prepared her to read it.

Can't say 100% until I get the skull, but I'm almost positive it's Jenna Mitchell.

Mechanically, she closed the message and stuffed the phone back into her pocket. Her mind whirred, but her heart closed itself off. Too many memories, too many regrets, too many things that should've happened differently.

How could this be her closest girlfriend from childhood, nothing but dried-out bones in plastic bags? And how much had she suffered?

"Laney?" The concern in Ryan's voice forced her to look up. "What is it?"

Her head went woozy, and she groped for the edge of the lab bench to steady herself.

He pulled up a stool, took her by the arms and forced her onto it. "You're white as a sheet. Sit."

"A text came from the Smithsonian. They think…"

His jaw set. "They think this is Jenna. I know."

"You do?"

"Not here—" he tapped his head "—but here." His hand pressed against his heart as moisture glistened in his chocolate-brown eyes. "I knew it the moment those teenagers brought the first bone in."

"They won't know for sure until we send the skull," she said faintly. "I'm so sorry, Ryan."

He seemed to blow off her words, blinking a few times before glancing at the pile of bags in the bin on the floor. "How much more time do you need here?"

She thought about pressing him—after all, if this discovery hurt her heart this badly, it had to be killing him. Surely he needed to process this loss with someone who understood.

But maybe she wasn't the right person for that job anymore. Maybe there was someone new in Ryan's life?

Ignoring how that thought made her feel, she pulled her gloves back on and removed the bone she'd been studying from under the microscope. "I've got the big stuff. The details need to be done in my lab, with better equipment."

"Good. Then let's pack these up and get you home."

A hard knot of determination formed inside her chest. Ryan and his team would still need her help sorting through the Wilson case files. And what if they combed the bog and found more remains? Leaving would be easier, by far, but she owed it Jenna to see this case through.

"No, I'm staying."

His brow furrowed. "No way, Laney. You're going. We can get your mom into a rehab program without you. It isn't safe for you here."

"It wasn't safe for Jenna, either, was it?" Tears pricked her eyes. "From what I've seen, her death wasn't an accident. I don't expect you to understand, but I owe her this. Send the bones. The other scientists in my lab are top-notch. They have my complete trust."

"You're right, I don't understand. You're being ridiculous, Laney. Jenna would never have wanted you to stay here if it was dangerous. We can always call in another forensics expert if we find more remains."

She bounced one knee impatiently. How could she make him understand without telling him what had happened the day Jenna disappeared? Because *that* was out of the question.

"Ryan, I'm asking you this as a favor. Please."

Those huge, soul-searching eyes had always been Ryan's weakness. That and the fact that he knew exactly how stubborn Laney could be once she'd made up her mind. Still, he couldn't give in *that* easily.

He placed both hands gently on her upper arms. "Someone is after you, Laney, and it goes beyond your expertise and what you might uncover about this case. There's something deeper going on, and until we figure out what it is, you'll be safer far away from here."

She shook her head—no surprise there. "Whoever it is knew where to find my childhood home and my mother. How easy would it be for them to track me down in DC, too? If somebody is after me, what makes you think I'd be any safer there?"

Much as he hated to admit it, she had a point. "We can coordinate your protection with a DC law enforcement unit."

"That'll never work, not if the killer is determined to get me. You know it."

"Don't have very much faith in us, do you?"

"I have a lot of faith in *you*. That's why I want to stay." The way her eyes softened made his insides melt, but was she just saying that to get him to cave?

He pressed his lips into a line. It wasn't likely any other officer would take guarding her as seriously as he would. Ryan let out a breath. "All right. But you're following my orders, got it? I can't protect you if you go off chasing your own headstrong ideas."

The smile that parted her lips lit up the entire room. "Thank you."

"Do we have a deal?" He held out his hand.

"Deal." She slipped her hand into his, sending a little tremor tickling up his arm. "What's next, partner?"

Good thing he knew better than to ever trust her with his heart again or else this new partnership would mean serious trouble. He pointed at the bin of remains. "I'll get somebody in here to box up the evidence and ship it to your lab. You and I are going to watch movies."

As he led the way back to his desk, Laney nodded toward the police chief's office. "When do we tell your dad?"

"About Jenna?" Her name snagged in his throat, and he swallowed. So hard to imagine that pile of mutilated bones had once belonged to his living, vibrant sister.

And what she'd had to endure—his stomach twisted,

but he couldn't let himself think about that, not now. Not when they had a killer to catch.

"And about me staying here," Laney added.

"We'll tell him about you later tonight, but I don't want to bring up Jenna until the forensic odontologist confirms the identification. It's going to be hard on my parents, but it'd be even worse if there was some kind of mistake."

"Of course." Empathy clouded her face. He'd always appreciated that about her—how she was so concerned for others and how much she had loved his parents.

He led the way to his office space and waved at Sergeant Ross, who sat behind one of the other desks. The other man was about his age but hadn't grown up here, so mercifully no comments followed about Ryan and Laney being together again.

Laney took a seat in the chair Ryan offered and waited as he flipped on his computer and pulled up the security footage.

"There are only twenty-seven hours to watch." He winked and was rewarded with a laugh. Every now and then, he'd catch a glimpse of the twinkle that used to live in her eyes despite everything she'd endured. It felt good to see it again.

"I *would* like to visit my mother in the hospital today."

"I know. And I need to ask her some questions. Let's start with the night you arrived. We'll follow your bag from unloading to when that guy brought it to you inside the terminal."

"That reminds me—did you get any footage on the bathroom attacker?"

"Yes, and we can look at that, too, though unfortunately we don't see much. They seemed to know where the cameras were pointed."

It took only a few minutes to review the recordings from the cameras outside the bathroom. Someone clothed in black, wearing a hoodie, slipped inside just after Laney entered. A second camera showed the same individual exiting into the other hallway a few minutes later.

"An airport employee might have insider knowledge about the cameras," Laney offered.

"Yes." Ryan drummed his fingers on his desk. "But it's not much to go on. Let's hope we get more from the other footage."

He opened the file for the security camera on the gate where her plane's passengers disembarked. The first several minutes showed nothing until the plane arrived and the ramp was attached to the door. A ground truck drove up, and two ramp agents climbed out, but the black-and-white footage was blurry and obscured their faces.

Laney pointed at the monitor. "That might be the man who brought me my carry-on. The height and posture look about right, but it's so grainy. Can you get it any clearer?"

"I wish. It's all about the video quality. But we can at least get names for who was on this shift." They kept watching as all the bags came off and were loaded on the truck. The handlers climbed into the cab and vanished off camera. "Then we have a gap in the coverage, where the bags are carted to the belt that takes them up to the claim area."

He loaded the next video in the sequence, showing the same workers tossing luggage haphazardly onto a conveyor belt. More than one suitcase toppled and was righted by one of them. The picture was clearer, but the angle was awkward, never showing either man's face.

When the video cut off, Laney said, "My bag wasn't there. It didn't go up onto the belt."

"Maybe it's on the next video for that camera." He pulled up the timestamp they needed, but the conveyor had gone still. One of the workers drove off in the truck. The other was already gone.

Laney leaned forward, resting her chin on her hand. "Where did it go?"

Ryan fast-forwarded through a few minutes in which nothing happened, but then movement in the corner of the frame caught his attention. "Wait, what's that?"

A worker moved back into range, but only his legs were visible. He lingered for a moment before walking off again.

"Was he getting mine?" Laney asked, pointing at the monitor. "Did they leave it behind on accident or something?"

"*Or something* is more like it," he said, pursing his lips. That moment off camera provided the perfect opportunity to stow an explosive device inside her suitcase without anyone noticing. "I'm skipping ahead to the footage inside the terminal when the employee brought you the carry-on. Maybe it was the same guy. This lens was angled at the baggage claim office."

For a long moment they stared at only an empty room, until Laney and the security guard appeared. Watching the way she jumped when that employee sneaked up on her made Ryan feel like punching the guy in the face. Too bad his back was to the camera.

"Turn around," Laney muttered under her breath. Onscreen, she took the suitcase's handle and the man finally turned, his face appearing for a fleeting second.

Ryan clicked his mouse to pause the video, then

backed up the frames one at a time until they had the clearest view of the man's face. "There. Recognize him?"

She nodded. "Now let's compare his face to the pictures in your files."

He opened the folder containing the most likely potential suspects and clicked through each file one at a time. They'd made it three-quarters of the way through the list when Laney pointed at one of the pictures. A nondescript man, maybe early fifties, with brown hair and hazel eyes stared back at them.

"That's him." She wrinkled her nose.

"Lawrence Brown, single, age fifty-two, Delta employee at Evansville Regional since 2007," Ryan read from the file. "Before that he worked at the BP station on the corner of Third and Smithville."

Hannah, the police department's admin assistant, poked her head in the door. "Hey, Sergeant Mitchell, the lab came back with an early analysis on the suitcase crime scene. I sent you the file."

"Already? Excellent." He clicked the computer mouse, changing the display to open the report. "Traces of ammonium nitrate, battery acid, steel, zinc, cell phone components. All things that could be procured by an amateur with a little bit of effort."

"So…" Laney stared across the room for a moment. "What if I'd listened to that threat and gotten right back on a plane? Would that bomb have gone off in the air?"

"No, it would've been detected when you went back through airport security, and you would've enjoyed a cozy night in jail while we tried to sort out what really happened."

"I guess that's something." A conspiratorial smile played at her lips. "Do we have an address for Lawrence Brown?" She'd never been one to shy away from trouble, that was for sure.

"Why, yes we do." He closed the report and stood. "Now all we need is a search warrant and one of our K-9 teams."

Laney dutifully followed Ryan around the station as he handled all the details with masterful precision. First stop had been updating the chief on what they'd learned from the video footage and lab report. Once he gave them permission to request the warrant, Ryan had tracked down Sandy Bluff's judge to get the actual approval, based on the evidence they presented. Last stop had been the K-9 unit, which in Sandy Bluff, amounted to two officers and their dogs. One was trained to detect drugs, the other to find explosives.

Fortunately for them, Officer Sarah McIntosh and her trusty German shepherd Marty were available to meet them at Brown's home in half an hour.

The house was down one of the many hilly, narrow roads crisscrossing the landscape to the northeast of Sandy Bluff, not all that far from the trailer park where Laney had grown up. She and Jenna had taken up cycling in their junior year of high school, in hopes of riding in the Little 500 race at IU. They'd traversed many of these country roads together until the day Jenna vanished.

Laney shuddered at the memory and at the view out her window. What had happened to Jenna that day? Had she gotten a flat tire, stopped to change it all alone? Or had a problem with her cell and knocked on a stranger's door to use the phone? Did the killer live in one of these houses?

Her stomach twisted, made worse by the gnawing

guilt that ten years hadn't erased. When Jenna had called to ask about riding, teenage Laney had been lying in bed, head hanging over a bucket, trying not to puke. Morning sickness, hard on the heels of a positive pregnancy test only a few days earlier. Less than three weeks since their high school graduation.

She'd panicked when she'd heard Jenna's voice. There was no way she could go out on a bike feeling like this without her friend knowing something was up. And the last thing she'd wanted to do was admit what she and Ryan had done. What the consequences would be. How could she have known the baby would miscarry a week later?

Instead, she'd spend a lifetime regretting the words she'd said next. *You go on without me, Jenna. This stomach bug feels like it might linger.*

Truth was, Jenna's death was ultimately her fault. And she could *never* let anyone find out. Especially Ryan.

Pushing aside the horrible thoughts, she glanced at him. "Any word on the getaway vehicle from yesterday?"

"No, not yet. But we'll find it." His expression was grim, his fingers tight on the steering wheel. If only she had the right words to ease some of that tension gripping his shoulders.

A few minutes later, Ryan slowed and turned into a long driveway on a flat lot. Officer McIntosh sat waiting behind the steering wheel of her SUV.

The house was a one-story ranch, all brick, with a roof that had seen better days and landscaping gone native. The front yard was mostly open to the road, but the sides and back were shrouded by tall deciduous trees. At the end of the driveway, a rusty white sedan was parked beneath the open carport.

"Looks like he's home." Laney pointed at the car.

Ryan waved at Officer McIntosh as she climbed out of her vehicle. "Sarah will handle the bomb-evidence search with Marty. You and I are going to find Mr. Brown."

"What if he recognizes me?"

He shrugged. "Then I'll get to see his reaction."

Clouds flitted across the sun, bathing the house and yard in shadow as they approached the front door. Laney drifted closer to Ryan. Both his strength and that sidearm in his belt made for good company at a moment like this, especially after what had happened to her and her mother at the trailer park. Even though it was heavy, wretchedly hot and uncomfortable, she was grateful for the bullet-proof vest Ryan had insisted she wear.

They waited until Sarah led Marty up to the front step, the German shepherd already sniffing intently in first one direction and then another, before Ryan pounded on the front door.

"Open up. Sandy Bluff police. We have a warrant to search this property."

The air was still, the only sound coming from Marty's collar as he nosed the ground.

"Car's in the driveway." Sarah tipped her head in the direction of the carport. "But maybe he isn't home?"

Ryan shrugged and hammered on the door again. "Open up. This is your last chance to cooperate before we force entry."

When no response came, he tried the knob. The door swung open with a creak straight out of a horror movie. Ryan moved aside to let the dog inside first, with Sarah holding the lead.

Laney followed the others, stopping on a peeling lino-leum entry inset in the carpeted living room. The place was sparsely furnished with a sofa table beneath the picture window overlooking the front yard, an orange plaid sofa that seemed like a relic from the 1970s and a flat-panel television above the brick fireplace. The few wall hangings were generic, as if they'd been borrowed from the nearest motel.

The dog paused at the break between the carpet and linoleum, sniffing the ground and the air. Sarah gave him a moment to acclimate to the new smells and then commanded, "Marty, search." Marty began working his way around the room, pausing now and again but not alerting. Yet, anyway.

It would be wonderfully convenient if Lawrence Brown was the bombing culprit. If they could get the evidence they needed and make the arrest, maybe he'd talk. Confess to his crimes and give up whoever had threatened her at the airport. Maybe he'd even reveal who had killed Jenna Mitchell. Laney could wrap up this case, knowing she'd done everything she could for Jenna, and head home before anything truly disastrous happened.

But now wasn't the time to get ahead of herself. First, they had to find Mr. Brown.

"Lawrence Brown?" Ryan called loudly. "This is Sergeant Ryan Mitchell with the Sandy Bluff Police. We need to ask you some questions, and we have a warrant to search your property."

Silence, broken by what sounded like a soft click somewhere in the recesses of the house. She glanced at Ryan, lifting her eyebrows in question. His dark eyes settled on hers as if to reassure her he was there, but instead of responding, he called out again.

"Mr. Brown?"

When no response came, he pulled his gun and a flashlight from his belt. Across the room, Sarah removed her firearm also as she followed Marty toward the kitchen.

Laney swallowed, suddenly highly aware of how unarmed she was. Why had she thought this was a good idea? Now Ryan had to protect *her* on top of trying to catch the suspect.

He raised a finger to his lips, gesturing for her to follow. She nodded, even though her heart had turned into a jackhammer inside her ribs, and tiptoed silently down the hall after him.

If the bomber was lying in wait down the hall, what kind of trap were they walking into?

SEVEN

Marty's soft sniffing faded from the range of Laney's hearing as she and Ryan advanced down the hall. Doorways opened off both sides into shadowy interiors, as if Mr. Brown never bothered opening his curtains to let in any daylight.

She shivered. Or he liked to keep the house dark to get the jump on police officers and forensic anthropologists.

At the first room, to the left, she flattened herself against the wall as Ryan stepped inside, gun up. The light came on as he flipped the switch before emerging again. She glanced in as they walked past—a bathroom, with the shower curtain pulled back to reveal an empty tub.

More thumps came from a room farther down, and her heart leaped up into her throat, but Ryan remained as steady and unflappable as ever. He'd been her rock in high school, too, a safe place to turn in the chaos of her life. Up until the moment everything had unraveled.

The worst part was, things hadn't needed to end up the way they had. Her and Ryan's relationship probably could've recovered from the intimacy they'd stolen if she hadn't gotten pregnant and been too terrified to tell anyone the truth.

Secrets always destroyed people in the end, didn't they?

She forced her thoughts back to the present as they entered the next room. It was empty, too, save for a futon, a stack of boxes and a desk covered in what appeared to be unopened bills.

Three doors were left, one of them shut.

Ryan pulled open the closed one to reveal a closet, and at the same moment, something flashed past Laney's feet.

She jumped, clamping a hand over her mouth to keep from screaming as a cat darted out of the closet and raced down the hall toward the living room. Tension ebbed out of her insides, making her knees weak. *That* must have been the source of the thumps. Lawrence Brown probably wasn't even home.

Ryan glanced back at her, a smile playing on his mouth.

A sharp hiss coming from the direction of the kitchen told her the cat had met Marty, but the trained police dog didn't bark. Sarah would be giving him extra treats tonight, no doubt.

The hall ended in a pair of doorways, both open but so dark inside she could barely make out the beds within. Ryan gestured for her to wait as he entered the one on the left, then disappeared into the darkness. The beam of his flashlight sent a long swath of light flicking across the room.

She let out a long, slow breath. Thank the Lord, they were almost done with this search. One room to go, and then there'd be nothing to do but recheck the rooms for evidence while Sarah and Marty finished their work.

Suddenly a dark shape materialized in the other doorway, the one Ryan hadn't checked yet, and wood dug sharply into Laney's back as she pressed against the frame. A man emerged wearing tattered overalls. Brown hair, hazel eyes and an unsettling look on his face as his gaze swept over her. The man from the airport.

A little yelp of surprise escaped her lips before she could stop it.

Ryan was at her side within seconds, and Sarah appeared with Marty at the far end of the hall, a frown darting across her features.

The man held up both hands, glancing between the officers before settling his gaze on Laney. His expression didn't quite seem right for the situation—not the stress or concern she would've expected—but almost a hint of a smile.

"Officers, can I help you?" he asked. "And I'd like to see your warrant."

Ryan kept the gun on him as he said, "We knocked and announced our arrival more than once. Why didn't you respond?"

"Didn't hear you." The man scratched his head. "I work late shifts and have to sleep at odd hours."

Ryan frowned but lowered his weapon. Down the hall, Sarah did the same, letting Marty continue sniffing his way toward them. "Are you Lawrence Brown?" he asked.

"That's me. But you can call me Larry." Something about him made Laney's stomach twist. Maybe it was the unnerving way his gaze stayed locked on her face. She resisted the urge to hide behind Ryan.

"We have a warrant to search your property, and you'll need to accompany us to the police station for questioning." Ryan held out the warrant for his inspection.

Brown barely glanced at it before fixing his gaze on Laney again, lips curling. "You're a lot prettier now than when you were little. Don't look much like your momma, though."

Her body went rigid as shock coursed through her system. He'd acted like she looked familiar at the airport, but—

Ryan interrupted her thoughts, shooting her a concerned glance as he spoke. "Mr. Brown, please keep your personal comments to yourself."

Sarah and Marty came out of the room containing the futons and boxes. Marty trotted up to the three of them and sniffed Brown with interest but then pushed past him into the bedroom. Sarah held the leash firm. "Marty, stay."

Brown glanced down at the dog. "Hey, pooch. What're you looking for? You won't find drugs here. I'm clean."

"We'll discuss it at the station," Ryan said. He extended a hand toward the living room. "You'll need to come with us."

When the man calmly walked in front of them back out to the police car, Laney couldn't decide whether she felt relieved or disappointed.

Ryan paced back and forth outside the one-way glass window of the interrogation room. Lawrence Brown sat comfortably on one of the hard metal chairs, sipping a cup of watery coffee and glancing periodically around the room. Every now and then, his gaze would fix on the mirrored glass as if he were trying to watch Ryan and Laney standing outside.

"How long are you going to make him sit there?" Laney asked. She seemed none the worse for the afternoon's unsettling experience, but she'd had quite a shock when Brown had appeared out of nowhere. Maybe Ryan could crack that tough exterior and get her to open up later tonight if they ever had an opportunity to take a break. Talking would help her handle the subtle psychological strain of being in jeopardy.

"We always let suspects wait before we come in. Sets them on edge." Though it didn't appear to be working, in this case. "Besides, Sarah took the dog to sniff the remains from your suitcase. He'll let us know if he picks up Brown's scent anywhere."

"But his house came up clean, didn't it?"

"Yeah, it did." Unfortunately. If Brown was their man and had managed to wipe the trace of explosives away, they'd have no case against him. Unless they could get a confession now. "If we can't get anything out of him, we'll have to release him."

"I know. Then it'll be back to watching security footage." She remained expressionless and stoic, but she had to be feeling *something*. After years of watching her put on a brave face at school but crumble in private, he'd learned to recognize both her strength and her need to be vulnerable with someone safe.

He almost checked himself—maybe she didn't view him as safe anymore—but they were partners now, and he needed to offer her reassurance. So he rested a hand lightly on her arm and squeezed ever so gently. "We'll find whoever is after you. Even if it's not him."

Laney rewarded him with a slight upturn of the lips. She held his gaze for a moment before she looked away again. "Thanks."

"Do you think he knew you as a kid? Or was he making that up?"

"I don't know." She chewed her lip for a moment. "But I have an idea. Let me think about it."

His radio crackled, and Ryan pulled it from his belt. "This is Mitchell."

"Ryan—" Sarah's voice *"—Marty isn't picking up his scent. We'll have to look elsewhere."*

"Thanks, Sarah." He swallowed his disappointment, nodded once at Laney and strode into the interrogation chamber.

Lawrence Brown raised a hand in salute, once to him and a second time to the window. "Sergeant. Where's that cute little Laney Hamilton? Watching from outside?"

He clenched his jaw. The guy may be clean, but the way he'd looked at Laney made Ryan want to punch him in the gut. Hard. But showing his emotions would only give the suspect the upper hand, so he pasted on a fake smile. "Mr. Brown, I have a couple of questions for you. Were you at work at Evansville Regional on the night of August 17? Two nights ago?"

"Sounds right to me." Brown slouched back in his chair, rolling the bottom of his paper coffee cup around in circles on the table. "I mean, if they schedule me, I show up. You can ask my boss."

"And was this you, bringing out a suitcase that somehow was left off the baggage claim conveyor belt?" He held up a hand and rotated his finger to cue the technician in the booth to play back the security video on the small television hanging in one corner of the room.

He watched Brown intently as the other man stared up at the screen, a smile flickering across his face as he startled Laney in the footage.

Brown pointed at the screen. "Guess I made an impression." He leered at the one-way glass, and Ryan winced on the inside.

No doubt Laney had seen that.

"What happened with the bag, Mr. Brown? Why did you need to bring it up to the claims office?"

"How else was she going to get it back? Taber and I unloaded the plane, like normal, but when I checked the dock, one bag had gotten left behind somehow. Protocol says to bring it to the claims office if the belt's been off fifteen minutes. You can check the airline's policy if you don't believe me."

Ryan pulled a notepad and pen out of his pocket, pausing for a long moment as he scribbled a line of notes on the paper. It wasn't necessary from the standpoint of his memory—he'd recall this unhelpful conversation just fine—but the action typically put suspects on edge.

Brown tapped the rim of his paper cup. "Can I get another cup of coffee?"

"When we're done." Ryan kept writing.

The other man leaned sideways and coughed into his elbow, intermittently at first, but working his way up into what sounded like a full-fledged case of emphysema. He pointed at the cup.

"Fine." Ryan snatched the cup and took it to the door, where Hannah was already waiting to go refill it. When she brought it back, he smacked it down on the table hard enough to slop dark droplets of liquid on the white surface.

Brown sat back up, a smirk dancing on his lips as he took a sip. "Ah, much better. Now, where were we?"

Ryan clenched a hand under the table. The coughing had been an act—he was sure of it.

He took his sweet time writing another page of nonsense before finally looking up. "During the time between the initial unloading of the plane and when you located the carry-on, how long would you guess it was left unattended?"

"Well…" Brown stared up at the ceiling for a moment.

"After we shut off the belt, Taber drove the truck back to maintenance, and I logged out the flight on the workstation computer. I found the bag about ten minutes later when I went back to sweep up."

"Huh." Ryan tapped his pencil on the table in as irritating of a fashion as he could. "I don't seem to recall seeing you sweep on the video footage."

"It's not literal sweeping. That's the janitorial staff's job. 'Sweep up' means we make a last pass to make sure we didn't miss anything."

"And that's when you discovered it?"

"Yep. And I took it straight to the claims office."

Ryan slowly rose to his feet, then pushed his chair back under the table. This interview was going nowhere fast, and unless he came up with something, they'd have to release Lawrence Brown. "I have to step out for a minute."

"Say hi to Laney for me."

She was waiting in the surveillance room along with the tech who controlled the video displays.

"That didn't go very well." Laney flopped onto a chair and tapped the armrests with her hands. "Do you think he's clean?"

"I don't know." Ryan paced back and forth in front of the one-way mirror. Inside the room, Brown sipped his coffee and glanced at his wristwatch. "My gut says he's involved, but we need hard evidence to detain him. And how does he know your name?"

"All I can think is that he must've had some connection with my mother." She frowned at the brown-haired figure on the other side of the glass. "What about the incident at the trailer park? Can you ask him where he was?"

"That line of questioning isn't directly related to

what's in the warrant, so we couldn't use anything he says as evidence. At least, not without jumping through the right hoops." He stopped in front of the glass, lost in thought for a moment. "But at least we might find out if that avenue is worth investigating."

He turned back at the doorway. "Laney, you don't have to watch. You can wait at my desk." Not only was Brown going out of his way to make her feel uncomfortable, but who knew what might come up during their conversation?

But she shook her head. Stubborn woman.

This time he brought a fresh cup of coffee when he walked in, just to keep the other man on his toes. "Here you go, Mr. Brown. Thought you might need another cup."

Brown held up a hand. "No thanks. Time for me to switch to decaf, or my tachycardia will act up." From the lazy smile on his face, he was enjoying every minute of this battle for control. Normal people didn't act this way when they were under investigation. They either cooperated and told the truth or sweated buckets as they lied and hoped no one figured it out.

No, Brown was the rare kind who enjoyed the struggle. Presumably because he was confident he'd win.

"Mr. Brown, where were you yesterday afternoon around four?"

"Getting ready for work. My shift started at six. It takes me an hour to drive there, park and get to my workstation."

"Can anyone confirm your whereabouts?"

"Dunno." Brown shrugged. "I live alone. The neighbors might've seen my lights on. Why do you want to know?"

Ryan wasn't ready to give up that information. He stood again. "Thank you. That's all for now."

"Can I leave yet? I have to work tonight."

"We'll be done soon," he answered from the door.

This time his father was waiting in the back room along with the others. The chief's expression was grim. "You're gonna have to let him go, Ryan."

"My gut says he's involved."

"I know, but your gut isn't admissible in court."

Laney laughed but clapped a hand over her mouth as Ryan shot her a glare. "What about the getaway truck?" she asked. "It wasn't at his house, but is a truck registered in his name? Or to someone connected with him?"

"I can check." The tech waved from behind a computer screen and clicked rapidly with the mouse. "No truck. Only a 2005 white Ford Taurus."

So much for that. He let out a slow breath. "Any other ideas?"

His father stepped past him, squeezing his arm gently on the way out. "I'm sorry, Ryan."

A minute later, Ryan stepped back into the interrogation room, this time holding the door open. "Thank you for coming down to the station, Mr. Brown. You're free to leave. One of the officers will give you a lift home unless you have other transportation."

"I've got a ride." Brown offered a pleasant smile that rang false to Ryan.

"You can collect your personal items at the front desk."

As Lawrence Brown walked to the front of the office, Ryan couldn't help wondering if he'd just released a killer.

EIGHT

Laney's mother was awake when she and Ryan finally made it to the hospital. On one hand, after the day she'd had, a family reunion was the last thing she wanted at this moment. But her mother might have vital information to reveal, and truth was, despite everything, Laney *did* care about her.

Being able to forgive her mother had been one of the many acts of grace God had performed in Laney's life, and she was forever grateful for His saving mercy.

"You ready?" Ryan asked. They'd stopped outside Kim Hamilton's door, watching as a nurse raised her mother's bed. He clasped her hand in his warm fingers and squeezed, and despite her better judgment, she squeezed too. He shouldn't be stepping back into this role as comforter, and she sure shouldn't be accepting his support. But there was no denying how nice it was not to carry this entire burden alone.

"As ready as I'll ever be."

The nurse stepped out, smiling at them as she passed. "She's ready to see you, but go easy on the questions, Sergeant. She's quite weak still."

Laney had almost forgotten Ryan was still in uniform—

somehow the blue shirt and dark pants seemed almost like an extension of who he was, rather than mere clothing. He might have joined the force mainly to please his father, but there was no doubt law enforcement was in his blood. She'd left her borrowed flak jacket back at the station after their unproductive visit to Lawrence Brown's house. *There* was a man she hoped she'd never see again.

She thanked the nurse and walked across the sterile white hospital floor to stand beside her mother's bed. Kim's eyelids fluttered at the sight of Laney, but she didn't smile.

"Elaine." Her voice was gravelly. "Why did you come back to this dead-end town?"

"Hi, Mom." Laney perched on the edge of a hard plastic stool as Ryan waited in the background, his presence like a solid anchor in the midst of emotionally rough seas. She wasn't sure what she'd expected her mother to say, but she *had* been hoping for something a bit kinder. "It's good to see you."

Kim's lower lip shook as if she were sucking on the inside of her cheek. "Go away, Laney. You shouldn't have come back here."

She hadn't thought her mother could possibly hurt her more, but judging by this sinking feeling in her chest, she'd been wrong.

For a second her mother and the hospital room vanished, and she was eight years old again, bouncing excitedly into their trailer after school only to find her mother passed out on the couch. The man Kim had brought home, another in a long string of transient, sometimes abusive boyfriends, laughed at Laney's crumpled little face.

The picture she'd so carefully drawn in art class for her mother fell from her hand.

And when she started to cry, he'd picked up the paper, balled it into a tight wad and tossed it in the trash.

She don't care what you made for her.

It was at that moment she'd decided never to let anyone see her cry again. Ryan had been the lone exception.

He stepped up beside her now, shaking her out of the memory. "Ms. Hamilton, she's here to help with a case. We have a few questions for you if you're up to it."

Kim squinted at him for a minute as if trying to identify him.

"I'm Sergeant Ryan Mitchell, from the Sandy Bluff Police. We're investigating the attack on you yesterday."

"You." She pointed a finger at him, her eyes narrowing. "What do you want with my daughter? She finally escaped this hole, and you lured her back, didn't you?"

Apparently her mother remembered him after all. Laney shook her head. "No, Mom. The police chief called me in. They found bones in the bog off County Highway 13. I'm a forensic anthropologist, remember?"

Her eyes lost their focus for a moment as she stared at the ceiling, muttering something incoherent under her breath. Ryan glanced at Laney, concern written across his features. No doubt wondering whether they should call back in a nurse.

"Not yet," Laney whispered. "She was probably high yesterday. Coming down still today."

When Kim finally turned back, she stretched her weathered fingers for Laney's hand where it rested on the bed. "I'm sorry, Laney. I'm so sorry. I was so proud of you making something of yourself. I should've told you not to come back."

She took the cold fingers in her own, swallowing her own sense of hurt and disappointment to be there for her mother. *God, please give her a second chance. Use this painful experience to change her life.* If nothing was impossible for God, even her mother wasn't too lost to be saved.

"Thanks, Mom," she said, "but you don't need to worry about me. I'm here for the job, and then I'll leave again. But you can help us by answering Sergeant Mitchell's questions."

Kim nodded, meekly subdued after her bitter outbursts.

"Can you tell us what happened yesterday?" Ryan asked. When she stared blankly at him, he added, "Or the last thing you remember before waking up here?"

"I had to work the 6:00 a.m. shift. I work at J's Discount Mart in case Laney didn't tell you. Been there nearly twenty years." Her voice carried a hint of pride. "Anyway, the next day I had off, so when I left at two, I swung by Cap n' Cork to pick up a bottle. Just to take the edge off. My doctor gave me antidepressants, but they don't work so good, so sometimes I drink too. You understand."

"Mom," Laney cut in, "tell us what happened."

"I am, I am. Quit bein' so impatient. I got back to the trailer an hour later and started drinking. After a couple of glasses, I laid down on the couch to take a nap. Then there was all this commotion at the door. Somebody pounding away. I figured it was Bernie wantin' his rent money, so I hauled myself off the couch to open the door. The last thing I remember is somebody dressed all in black shoving me backward."

"What about calling me, Mom? Do you remember calling me?"

"Did I? Wait a minute…" Her eyes unfocused for a

moment, then she blinked. "Yes, he pressed a phone to my ear. Told me to ask you for help."

"Do you have any idea who it might have been?" Ryan asked.

"No." Kim tried to shake her head but winced. "I don't know what he wanted either. Better notta taken my TV."

Laney squeezed the frail fingers. "It was still there. I'll keep an eye on everything for you. But we won't know if they took anything until you're well enough to go home."

"Ms. Hamilton, do you know a man from Sandy Bluff named Lawrence Brown?" Ryan asked.

"Larry Brown?" A puzzled expression flitted across her face. "Is that who you mean?"

Laney cringed inside at the casual way her mother said his name. Ryan pulled out a photograph he'd brought from Brown's employee record with Delta and showed it to her mother.

She frowned. "He lived with us for a couple of months, back when Laney was maybe twelve or thirteen. It was nice havin' a man around to help, and he had a steady job, but I didn't like the way he looked at her sometimes."

"Did he ever try to hurt you or Laney?" Ryan's tone had gone brittle.

"No. Just seemed a little…off, if you know what I mean. He put up a bit of a fuss when I told him to leave, but we didn't need a restraining order or nothin'."

Laney nibbled the inside of her lip, struggling to remember which of her mom's boyfriends had been around when she was in middle school. She did vaguely recall a blowout fight in the street outside the trailer. Her mom tossing clothes out the window. A man hammering on the door until the neighbors threatened to call the cops. Was that Lawrence Brown?

Ryan grazed his fingers against her lower back—a whisper of a touch, meant to offer support. He'd always been her rock in the midst of her mother's drama. He nodded at Kim. "Okay, thanks, Ms. Hamilton."

"When can I get out of here?" her mother asked.

Laney patted her hand. "Mom, that's something I need to talk to you about. I'm checking you into a rehab center as soon as they release you here. You have to sign the paperwork for consent, but I want you to do this now, while you still can."

Her mother stared out the window for a long moment. When she turned back to Laney, tears glistened in her eyes. "You've always been stronger than me."

"Not always, Mom. But God is good, and He takes care of those who love Him."

"When did you get into church?"

"In college." The tips of her ears flamed as she thought about Ryan standing there next to her, hearing her testimony. His fingertips rested lightly on her shoulder— meant to encourage, but they might as well have been bits of hot charcoal for the way they burned through her shirt. "I met some pretty amazing women who loved the Lord and shared His gift of forgiveness and salvation with me." She took a deep breath and plunged on. "You can have that gift, too, Mom. There's no sin too big, no past too ugly for God's grace."

Her mother blinked rapidly a few times, then turned back to the window. "I'm tired. Can I rest now?"

A lump lodged in Laney's throat, and she swallowed it back down. Hopefully she'd at least planted a seed in her mother's heart. *You can use even the most seemingly hopeless conversation, can't You, God?* Getting her into rehab after they released her from the med-surg unit would be a step in the right direction.

Ryan stayed close beside her as they navigated the maze of the hospital and found his car in the parking lot. Did he think she might break? That she wasn't strong enough to handle seeing her mother again?

Any doubts were dispelled by his words as he turned on the car's ignition. "You handled that really well. It could've gotten ugly."

That lump came back into her throat. "It *was* ugly."

"But you offered her forgiveness and hope, Laney." Instead of backing out, he fixed his dark eyes on her, and the respect she found in his gaze filled her insides with a confusing tangle of warmth and fear. His strength and encouragement mattered far more to her than they should.

She turned away and stared out the window at the empty car next to them. Anything to avoid those pensive eyes trying to read her soul. "It's been a long couple of days. Can we call it a night?"

"Absolutely. Let me take you home."

To Jenna's room, in Ryan's childhood home. The place was embroiled in regret and bittersweet memories, and yet Laney's shoulders relaxed on their own at the thought of going back. It had always been home to her, a safe haven in a world of chaos. If only everything could've stayed that way.

By the time he pulled into his parents' driveway, Ryan desperately wanted to get the details on the crime scene investigation from Kim Hamilton's trailer and to start following up on the other possible suspects for the airport bombing. But leaving Laney alone with his mother wasn't safe for either of them, and if he were being honest, he *wanted* to stay here with her.

He parked in the driveway and let Laney in through the side door from the garage to the house. A waft of some delicious smell made his mouth water almost instantly. Roast beef and potatoes, maybe?

Laney's eyes twinkled as she took off her shoes. "Remember that time we volunteered to cook dinner for your family? And you thought it'd be smart to grill the pot roast?"

"Hey, that meal was your idea. I wanted to order pizza."

"That would've been cheating," she countered, pointing a shoe at him.

"But it would've tasted a whole lot better." His heart felt lighter as he followed her into the kitchen. Good to know the happy memories still lurked in Laney's brain and that she hadn't forgotten them in her attempt to escape the bad ones.

He'd guessed right—his mother glanced up from a pan of potatoes, masher in hand, as he and Laney entered the room.

"Wonderful!" she exclaimed. "You two are back just in time for supper. Ryan, fetch everyone a glass of water. Laney, can you set the table?" She tipped her head toward the breakfast nook on the far side of the kitchen, with its sliding glass door letting in the late afternoon sunshine. "I'm sure you remember where everything is."

Laney's cheeks tinged pink, but she didn't hesitate to jump right in and help. As Ryan pulled drinking glasses out of the cupboard, he couldn't help thinking how it felt like old times. Jenna was the only one missing. If she could see them from heaven, she'd be smiling right now.

Mary scooped the potatoes into a large blue bowl and

placed them at the center of the table as Laney laid out the silverware. "How's your mother, honey?"

"She's recovering. Honestly, as hard as it is, I think this could end up being positive for her. A social worker is going to help me get her into a treatment program."

Ryan set the glasses down on the table, weaving between the two women. He hadn't enjoyed being at home this much in a long time.

His mother reached for Laney's hand. "We'll help out any way we can. I know you'll probably need to get back home eventually."

Back to DC. The thought felt like a bucket of ice water thrown over his head. Not that it was a surprise—he knew she couldn't stay here. Wouldn't. And, he reminded himself, that was a good thing.

Laney was like a butterfly who'd escaped her chrysalis to become something bigger and more beautiful. Trying to trap her here again would only crush her wings.

Sometimes over the past ten years, he'd wondered what would've happened if she'd stayed. Or if he'd tracked her down at Indiana University that first year after she left. Would she have resented him for the rest of their lives? Things had worked out for the best, and even though he hadn't succeeded at moving on, it didn't mean anything needed to change.

"Thanks, Mary." Laney set down a stack of plates and accepted a hug from his mother. He turned away, retreating deeper into the kitchen to give the women a moment without him hovering nearby.

As he leaned against the counter, his phone buzzed. It was a text from Hannah at the station. She'd been looking into the other baggage handlers who'd worked Laney's flights. She had three more names for him—Karen Martin, Eddie Reynolds and Dennis Taber. Two lived and worked up in Indianapolis, but Dennis Taber had been Lawrence Brown's coworker in the surveillance footage.

He wrote a quick response, telling her to pass along the Indy suspects to a detective he knew in that precinct. As for Dennis Taber... Sarah and Marty would help decide if he deserved their attention.

A soft click told him the door from the garage had opened, and a moment later his father walked into the kitchen. "Smells great in here. Did I miss dinner?"

Ryan pocketed his phone. "Hey, Pop, just in time."

Jim Mitchell threw his keys into a basket on the counter and ran a hand over his short hair. He glanced at the women in the breakfast nook, then asked in a low voice, "What did Laney learn about the remains?"

Right, *that*. He let out a sigh. "Bone sizes and growth indicate a female, probably in her late teens. Time of death between eight and twelve years ago."

Jim's throat bobbed as he swallowed. "Did you tell your mother?"

"No." He held up a hand. "Remember, it was only a preliminary exam. She can't say for sure until the bones are back in her lab and they compare the dental records."

He nodded. "Of course."

"Hey, I'm thinking about heading back into work tonight to see what evidence they've processed from the trailer park. Do you think you could make sure she stays safe?" He glanced back at Laney, whose dark hair bounced around her ears as she bent over to lay a fork beside one of the plates. Somehow she'd gotten only more beautiful with time.

"She'll be safe with us, son."

His mother walked back into the kitchen, greeted Jim

with a kiss and pulled the roast out of the oven. The glorious smell of beef and onions made Ryan's mouth water. "Go have a seat, you two. Time to eat."

They'd replaced the old table with one that sat four, and Ryan took a seat between his mother and Laney, opposite his father. Jim bowed his head to say the blessing, but Mary interrupted, "Can we hold hands for grace? It's so nice to have Laney back with us."

Obligingly, he offered Laney his hand, holding his breath for a moment as he waited to see if she'd take it. But of course she wouldn't want to hurt his mother, so she slid her petite hand into his—still a perfect fit. He ignored the warm feeling coursing through his insides. *Not* helpful.

As soon as his father finished praying, she pulled her hand away so fast she nearly knocked over her water glass.

"Tell us what you've been doing with yourself all these years, Laney," Jim said as he scooped potatoes onto his plate.

Her pale cheeks had never been able to hide a blush. She'd always been reluctant to talk about herself, and this awkward situation certainly hadn't improved things.

"We've had a long day, Dad," he intervened. "She might want to relax instead of sharing her life story."

The funny thing was, her life story would've included him for more than half of it. They'd met in first grade when their desks had been paired together. Ryan was still convinced the teacher had thought she'd be keeping him out of trouble by seating him with a girl. Instead, they'd started scheming practical jokes before the first month was out.

"No, it's okay." Laney smiled, though he could see

the weariness edging her eyes. "It's not that exciting, really. Four years of undergrad. Four years for my PhD. Then the Smithsonian hired me two years ago. If I can impress them enough, they might keep me on in a permanent position."

"Do you like living in DC?" Mary asked.

Laney pushed around the food on her plate with her fork. "I like...having my own place. And a prestigious job in a profession I love. It's nice to have that sense of security."

She didn't mean it as a slight against him, of course, but Ryan couldn't help wishing he could've been the one to provide her that sense of security. How often he'd wanted to rescue her from her life here yet been powerless to do so.

And now that he *could* be there for her, they could never go back.

Laney cleared her throat. "What's been happening here? Mom shared on Facebook they expanded the animal shelter?"

Changing the subject—a classic Laney trick. She knew his mother well. Mary latched onto the new topic with ardor, especially as she'd served as a "foster mom" for several litters of kittens and stray puppies over the years.

By the time dinner ended and they'd cleaned up the dishes, the sun's dying rays shaded his parents' back deck in hues of pink and orange and purple. He needed to get going, but watching Laney wander out to the deck alone tugged at his heart to follow.

His parents migrated out of the kitchen and into the living room, leaving him space to decide. As if there ever *was* a choice when it came to Laney.

She stood overlooking the backyard, where the green grass of his parents' large lot rolled down into thick woods and then eventually into another neighborhood, but the summer foliage blocked any other sign of humanity. Even the neighbors' houses weren't visible from back here.

He stood beside her, bracing both hands on the railing, close enough to sense her presence but not invade her space. She glanced up at him, offering a tiny smile. Cicadas hummed in the trees, and the air held that sultry, earthy smell of a late-summer night.

There were so many things he wanted to ask her—*why did you leave? Was it because of Jenna? Us?*

The rift between them felt wider than ever. As if her being back here and yet being so far away still meant they could never reconnect. God could redeem broken relationships, but some things were better left unresolved, weren't they?

So instead of letting out the thoughts burning in his heart, Ryan stared down at his hands. "I'm going to run downtown for a couple hours. See what they found at your mother's trailer." The words stuck in his throat like putty, as if his body were subconsciously rebelling against his choices. *Tough.*

She lifted an eyebrow. "Do you want me to come?"

"No, you stay here and rest. You need some sleep."

"All right. Thanks, Ryan." She smiled again, but her eyes still held that same weariness. Or was it unhappiness? Did being around him make her sad? Or maybe it was being back here in this mess and facing all the things she'd left.

He wished he could pull her into a long embrace, her cheek pressed against his chest as he held one hand against her head. But no matter how appealing that image was, he wasn't stupid enough to act on it.

No, Laney had made it clear Ryan wasn't what she needed anymore.

So, he ignored the silent plea of his heart and headed back to the one thing he'd always been able to count on—work.

NINE

The police station was quieter at night, a fact Ryan had always appreciated. Occasionally an officer investigating a case worked late, but usually only the night patrol officers were here. The city didn't pay overtime, so any detective work invested off-hours came purely from the generosity of their hearts. It had been hard to swallow at first—heading home to relax when so many things were left undone. But if he burned out, then even fewer crimes would be solved.

The evidence from Kim Hamilton's trailer had already been cataloged and stored in the evidence room. Ryan pulled up the report on his computer, scanning the list of items collected and notes made by the officers at the scene. Blood samples from the floor and the wall had been collected, though he had no doubt they'd match Laney's mother. No fingerprints on any of the surfaces, but that wasn't a surprise either. Laney said the man had been wearing gloves.

Kim Hamilton had let the intruder in through the front door, so there wasn't any evidence of forced entry. The culprit had apparently left the same way, then lay in wait for Laney to arrive.

The crime scene unit had also created a cast of one of the tire tracks from the getaway vehicle. Despite the dusty conditions, enough of an imprint had remained to get a partial one. With no DNA evidence, that truck could be a key piece of evidence.

Overall, though, there wasn't much to go on. And while he was convinced the airport bomber and the assailant on Kim Hamilton were one and the same, no proof could point him in the right direction.

And did any of this tie in with Lawrence Brown or Ronald Wilson?

He drummed his fingers on the desk for a long moment, debating what to do next. Probably going home to bed was the wisest choice, but he couldn't sleep right now, not with a threat to Laney's life on the loose.

What if he called the state prison system to check on Ronald Wilson? Wilson hadn't killed Jenna, but he might know something about the latest disappearance. Maybe the prison warden would know if he'd had new outside contact lately or if there'd been any suspicious activity.

It was late, but Ryan could at least leave the man a message. He pulled up Wilson's file, verified the name of the correctional facility and found the contact information for the warden. The phone rang a couple of times before voice mail picked up. He left a quick message, then hung up.

Probably time to give this case some space on his corkboard. After shuffling some papers to create a blank corner, he pinned up pictures of the hotel bombing and Kim Hamilton's trailer. Then the missing girl, just in case her disappearance was linked, and two cold cases—Jenna and the girl who'd disappeared a year afterward. His sister smiled at him from her senior picture, her dark hair shiny and thick against brown skin. Likely she would've been married by now, bringing a ragtag bunch of little nieces and nephews into the station to visit him.

He swallowed. Not sure he'd be able to keep her picture up there for long.

The phone rang when he was on the brink of heading home. Caller ID showed it was from Michigan City. The warden already?

"Sergeant Ryan Mitchell," he said as he answered.

"Mitchell, this is Bob Butler, warden at Indiana State Prison. I'm returning your call about Ronald Wilson."

"Excellent." If the warden had gotten back this fast, maybe he had something helpful to add to this case.

"Wilson's dead. He was attacked in the yard and beaten to death two months ago."

Two months…well before the college student disappeared or these attacks on Laney. Guess that confirmed Wilson wasn't involved.

"Okay, thanks." Ryan hung up the phone and sat staring at the corkboard. At Jenna and another innocent teen girl, this one with blond hair and a dental retainer across her smile. And at missing student Madison Smith, whose mother had broken down weeping at the police station.

If Ronald Wilson wasn't responsible, who was?

Laney hated the hollow feeling that had settled inside her chest. Being here with Ryan's family only painted a sharp contrast with the way things used to be back when she and Ryan had been inseparable and Jenna was her other best friend. Funny how, as twins, they'd been so different and yet Laney had loved them each dearly. Their whole family had filled the gap for everything that had been missing in her life—stability, parents, a sister, a boyfriend who loved her.

Until it was gone.

She stared out over the deck railing. Sometimes people blamed God for the bad things that happened in their lives, but in this case, Laney knew better. It was all her fault. But no amount of regret could change the choices she'd made.

So instead of dwelling on it, she needed to make the most of the few days she had to help Ryan and his family and then get back to her own life. She patted her hands lightly on the railing a couple of times before heading through the slider and into the house. Earlier in the day, Ryan had emailed her the case files for Jenna, the other cold case from a year later and those referencing Wilson's victims. Maybe if she looked them over before bed, she'd discover some new connection or angle to pursue.

Mary and Jim Mitchell sat in the living room, heads bent together over what looked like a crossword puzzle. How many years had they been married now? Must be going on thirty or even more. She couldn't recall how old they'd been when the twins were born.

Maybe that kind of love wasn't meant for everyone to find. She'd learned to be content living alone—maybe that was the life God had for her, not the beautiful relationship of Ryan's parents, which time had refined and polished into pure gold. Her heart twinged uncomfortably at the thought, because the one man she'd ever envisioned growing old with was definitely out of the question.

Mary waved her over as she passed through the room. "Come join us, Laney. We need help with 37 Down— 'Country that gave up its coastline in the War of the Pacific.'"

"I can get you the answer in less than fifteen seconds." Jim reached for his cell phone.

"That's cheating and you know it. Laney, we need your help."

She smiled but shook her head. "Thank you, but I'm beat after the day we had." She jerked a thumb toward the guest room. "I'm going to turn in early tonight."

"All right, dear. We won't be up too much later either."

The plush carpet felt soft against her feet as Laney walked the familiar path to Jenna's room turned guest room. The furniture was all new—a cherry sleigh bed, in place of the white canopy bed Jenna had had since she was seven, and a new matching chest of drawers and nightstand. Even the walls had been repainted. Part of it made Laney sad, but at the same time, she was glad the Mitchells had made an effort to move on. How hard it was to let go of the past.

Laney flopped down on the soft raspberry-hued comforter and downloaded the files Ryan had sent onto her laptop. The first was one of the Wilson cases, the one that had brought his conviction after the remains were discovered in a dumpster behind a gas station. The girl, who'd been only twenty years old, stared back at her from a photograph taken shortly before her death. She wasn't particularly pretty, but something about her eyes made her seem sweet and innocent. She hadn't deserved the fate she'd received at a killer's hands.

Laney opened a new tab and clicked through pictures of the remains. A shudder rippled across her shoulders as one after another crossed the screen. More than bones remained in this case—the girl had been missing only three months when they'd found her. The medical examiner's report indicated she'd been dead at least a couple of weeks before she was dumped. Bits of twigs and leaves in her hair suggested the body had been kept outside for some period of time.

Downsizing the gruesome pictures, she found the detailed list of evidence. The leaves had come from oak and hickory trees but hadn't borne any markers that could provide a more specific location. The bones had been cleaned and documented, and the file included close-ups of all the shearing marks and the damage to the skull used in court as evidence against Ronald Wilson.

A thump out in the hallway made Laney flinch. She sat silent for a long moment, listening, until she heard soft voices. Mary and Jim. They must be heading to bed.

She let out a long breath. Looking at files like these was sure to make a person jumpy. Still, she couldn't help hoping Ryan would be back soon. His father was the police chief and his house was secure, but nobody made her feel as safe as Ryan could.

What time was it anyway? A quick glance at the clock showed she should be going to sleep, too, but the thought of lying here in the dark wasn't exactly appealing. No doubt Ryan would be back any minute.

At the sound of a car outside, she slid off the bed and peeked through a crack in the wooden louvered blinds, out at the street beyond the front yard. Streetlights glowed orange down the length of the road, illuminating a neat row of wooden mailboxes and manicured lawns. The Mitchells lived on one of Sandy Bluff's better streets.

When no car turned into the driveway, Laney went back to her files. Wilson's other two victims had been found buried—not in Waltman's Bog, but in another field a few miles farther east. Both sets of remains had been reduced mainly to bone after two and four years buried in the mud. A cursory glance at the images of the cut marks showed they did appear to have been caused by the same implement, applied with similar force and direction.

Wait a minute... She sat up, fingers resting lightly against one particular image of the inferior end of a femur. Wilson had cut through the ligaments binding the bone to the patella, leaving marks on the rounded surface of the bone. She'd seen similar marks only that morning, when examining Jenna's remains.

Of course, joints were a natural place to dismember a body, but—

She flipped through the other images, diving into the other files to examine the remains from the other bodies. Then pulled out her cell phone, where she'd stored snapshots from her examination of the bog remains that morning.

There were variations in the blade's pattern, indicating different weapons used on Jenna compared to the others, but the angle of application and the force were essentially the same. Laney dropped the phone, pressing cold fingertips to her lips.

The same person who'd cut up these bodies had also dismembered Jenna Mitchell.

Ronald Wilson had been framed.

With a scraping sound, the Mitchells' air conditioner kicked on. Even though Laney recognized the noise, she shivered anyway.

Wait... Had she forgotten to lock the glass slider to the backyard? Her heart thumped a little harder, but she forced her shoulders to relax. No sense in panicking.

She closed her laptop and set it on the nightstand, sitting for a moment on the edge of the bed. It was tempting to climb under the covers and pull the comforter up over her head, but she'd never be able to sleep if she thought there was even a possibility the door was unlocked. Not that anyone would try to sneak into the police chief's house, but still…

Better safe than sorry.

The hallway was dark except for the soft green glow of a smoke detector down by the master bedroom. She stretched fingertips out to run along the wall on one side, feeling her way back to the opening into the living room. Up ahead, where the living room opened into the kitchen, faint light emanated from the clocks on the microwave and stove.

She stopped at the end of the hall, lingering for a moment in the relative safety of close walls. From here, a right-hand turn would take her through the open living room, past the door to the basement and into a formal dining room turned home office. Or if she followed the glow of the clocks, she could go a bit farther and turn through the kitchen.

Did it matter? It wasn't like anyone was *inside* their house. She was being ridiculous.

Still…she'd feel better with a weapon. The fireplace pokers sat a few feet away—the faintest hint of light reflected off the brass. She edged toward the metal stand, sliding sweaty fingers around the handle of the nearest one. The air stirred, the slightest breeze wafting across her face. Was it the vent? The air conditioner was still blowing.

She withdrew the poker, wincing at the grating sound as it rubbed against the stand. Maybe it would make more sense to go wake up Jim. He had a firearm after all.

But what would she say? *Jim, I think I forgot to lock*

*the sliding door to the backyard, and I'm too paranoid
to check it myself.* Ha, *that* wouldn't be embarrassing.

The brass poker felt heavy and reassuring in her hand,
and she ran her fingertips along the other end to make
sure she'd gotten the one with the sharp tip. *Perfect.* De-
ciding to go through the kitchen, she pushed on across
the living room carpet, feeling for the sofa table behind
the couch before she rammed a hip into it. A few more
paces brought her to the wall dividing the kitchen from
the home-office space, and she navigated around the cold
granite countertop by the light of the microwave clock.

One hand on the kitchen island guided her to the end
of the room and the breakfast nook where they'd had dinner. On the far side of the table, the floor-length linen
curtains hanging over the slider were closed.

A breath of relief escaped her lips. She didn't remember pulling them together, but she must have done it when
she'd shut the doors. Either that, or Mary had before
heading for bed.

She turned to go but froze when movement caught
her eye. One of the curtains at the far end of the table
was fluttering ever so slightly, as if caught in a breeze. It
had to be the air conditioner blowing—surely there was
a floor vent against the wall—but she tightened her grip
on the poker anyway.

Edging around the table and chairs, she tiptoed across
the hardwood floor closer to the moving curtain. The
only way to check for a vent was to pull the curtain
back—like a scene straight out of a low-budget horror
movie.

The panicky part of her felt like screaming, the rational part like laughing. Good thing nobody was around
to watch.

Her fingers grazed the thick linen fabric until she found the edge of the curtain. A breeze danced across her skin, making goose pimples stand up on her arms. It wasn't cold enough to be air-conditioning, was it?

Swallowing, she pulled the fabric back to reveal the floor. There was no vent.

The sliding glass door was open.

TEN

Laney's heart launched into her throat as she stared at the open space where safe, *locked* glass should have been. Something thumped nearby—much too close—and she spun around with the poker in hand, opening her mouth to scream.

But the sound was muffled as a dark mass pressed into her face, soft and smothering like a heavy sweatshirt, shoving her sideways and backward against the glass door. Her assailant yanked the poker out of her hand and dropped it onto the floor with a loud clatter.

Lord, please let that be enough to wake Jim!

She flung both hands up to claw at the sweatshirt, struggling to free her face and suck in a breath of air. The fabric rammed into her nose and mouth, making it hard to breathe.

Her assailant was bigger and stronger, and even though she kicked and scratched, he easily threw an arm around her neck and dragged her toward the open door. If he got her out of the house… Ryan and Jim would have no idea where to look for her.

Flailing for the door, she clamped her fingers to the

metal edge of the slider and managed to hook one foot around the inside.

The man grunted and strained against her as he half shoved, half pulled her out of the house. She twisted in his grasp, struggling with every ounce of energy, until her other foot connected with part of his leg.

He groaned, his grip loosening just slightly, and Laney kicked again. Somewhere close by, a car engine roared onto the street, the sound just audible above the man's grunts and Laney's frantic thumping. His arm tightened around her neck, squeezing shut her airway. Panic flared beneath her ribs, and out of sheer instinct, she dug her nails viciously through his shirtsleeve into his skin.

More thumping sounds came from inside the house now, and she was sure she heard a door slam.

Out here! Her brain tried to scream the words as stars flared in her vision. *Please, Lord, let them find me.*

She lost her grasp on the sliding door and the man yanked her out onto the deck. The sweatshirt still covered her head, but the feel of the air shifted. Somewhere beyond their struggle, a few stubborn cicadas made their last evening calls. Her assailant relaxed his arm enough to let her draw in a precious gasp of air as he dragged her toward the steps that would lead down into the yard.

"Stop!" Ryan's voice broke the silence of the night, sending a wave of relief crashing through Laney's tense body.

For a split second, her assailant tightened his grip as if he were going to attempt to flee with her. She twisted beneath his arm, digging into his skin again, until he abruptly yanked the sweatshirt away from her face and let her go. The sudden release made her lose her balance, and she crashed down onto the wooden deck, the edges of the boards biting into her palms.

The man thundered down the steps and out into the yard. Ryan didn't hesitate.

"Wait here," he ordered. As if she was in any fit state to follow. Without waiting for a response, he vaulted over her legs and hurdled down the stairs after the attacker, chasing him into the dark night.

Laney rolled onto her back and stared up at the summer stars overhead, sucking in a couple of deep breaths. A moment later, Jim ran out of the open door. His feet pounded across the wooden deck and he knelt beside her.

"Laney, what happened? Are you all right?"

She propped herself up on her elbows, letting out another shaky breath. "Yeah, I think so."

"Here, let me help you up." He took one of her hands and hoisted as Laney climbed to her feet. Her legs had turned to jelly. Back inside, Jim flipped on the pendant light over the dining table and helped her onto one of the chairs. He was dressed in plaid pajama pants and a blue T-shirt, and from the rumpled look of his hair, he'd been asleep only minutes before. "I heard noises out here on the deck. What happened?"

She pressed chilled, trembling fingertips against her temples, glad for something to talk about to distract her from thinking. Because it would be later, when she was alone and had to deal with what had happened, that she'd pay the true price. "I was awake in my room, reading case files, when I realized I forgot to lock the door after I came in earlier. A man jumped me—" a lump formed in her throat "—before I could scream for help."

"Here? In the house?"

"Ryan scared him off. He's pursuing him now on foot."

Jim's face settled into a hard scowl, and he pulled the sliding door shut, locking it securely into place with the drop-down security bar. "I'm going to get Mary and then help Ryan."

His wife, wrapped in a fleece bathrobe, bustled into the kitchen. "I'm already awake. I'll see to Laney. You go."

Jim strode out of the kitchen, flipping on more lights in the back hallway as he went. The jingling of keys reached Laney's ears, followed moments later by a car's engine.

Mary pressed both hands to her mouth and shook her head as she turned to Laney. "Oh, my poor girl. I heard everything." She walked over and cupped Laney's cheeks in her hands. Then placed them on her head and bent over to kiss her forehead.

The lump in Laney's throat turned into tears, which she blinked back as best she could. "I'll be okay," she said. Both to put on a brave face and because it was true. She'd gotten through a lot of awful things in her life. She'd make it through this experience too.

"Let me get you some tea." Mary walked back to the counter and set to work filling an electric tea kettle and pulling out a couple of mugs. She put a basket of tea bags on the table in front of Laney.

Chamomile sounded soothing. Laney pulled one out and tore open the small package. Was her attacker the bomber himself? Or, worse, a serial killer?

A few minutes later, Mary set a steaming mug of water before her, too, and took the opposite seat. "It's been so nice having you back, Laney, but I wish these terrible things would stop happening to you."

"I'm just glad you and Jim were safe." What an awful thought, that she could be putting their lives in danger too.

Mary smiled, her expression tainted by sadness. "I'm married to a cop. Danger comes with the territory."

"Your family has suffered enough already." Laney curled her cold fingers around the hot mug. The warmth soaked into her palms, soothing and comfortable.

"That's why it means so much to have you back again. You've always been like a daughter to me." The skin around Mary's brown eyes crinkled as she smiled again. Then she glanced down at her mug and stirred in a spoonful of sugar. Her next words came a bit too slowly. "I know why you left, Laney."

Laney's throat closed. How could she possibly know about the miscarriage? Laney hadn't told *anyone*, not even Jenna. And certainly not Ryan. She was sure her face had gone white as a sheet, and to cover the reaction, she sipped at her tea.

Mary sighed. "With the way your mother treated you, it was only to be expected you'd want to get away. But you could've moved in with us. You've always been welcome here."

Air whooshed back into Laney's lungs. Mary didn't know she'd nearly been a grandmother. Laney pressed a hand to her chest, her heart beating double time beneath her fingers, and smiled warmly. "I know, Mary. I've always felt so at home here. But I needed to get away from Sandy Bluff. Start with a clean slate. I know I hurt your family, and I'm so sorry, but I wouldn't be where I am today if I'd stayed."

Mary reached across the table to lay her hand on Laney's. "I understand, and I know God is at work in your life like He is in Ryan's. Good will come in the end."

Did she think that good would somehow involve Laney and Ryan getting back together? Because Laney was pretty confident it would never happen. If Ryan knew why she'd really left, he'd never forgive her. None of them would. Why taint what positive memories they had left?

By the time his father pulled up in the car, Ryan had given up the chase. It wasn't the running—he was in great physical shape—but the suspect must've mapped out the entire neighborhood, because he'd known every shortcut, every detour that led away from streetlights and porch lights, until he'd vanished into the beltline of forest that ran between the neighborhoods.

He'd probably approached the Mitchells' home that same way, from the woods in the back. First thing in the morning, they'd get a team into the forest to search for footprints, though with how dry it had been lately, Ryan had little hope of finding anything conclusive.

Jim rolled down his window as Ryan stood at the end of the street, staring between the houses and into the woods. "Want a ride?"

He rubbed a hand over his jaw, hating to give up, but the search would be fruitless at this point. "Sure."

As soon as he climbed into the passenger seat, Ryan reported the suspect on his radio to alert any officers in the area to be on watch.

"Did you get any visual on him?" Jim asked.

"Five ten, I'd guess, less than two hundred pounds. Physically fit enough to get away, but he had his escape route mapped. Though he'd have had a hard time dragging Laney all that way…" Despite how petite she was. The man must've had a different route planned for if he'd gotten away with her. His stomach twisted at the thought.

"Clothing?"

"Looked like dark jeans and a hoodie, but no identifying features. Maybe I'll walk the route back to our house. Just in case there's a clue." He pulled out a flashlight from his utility belt.

Jim nodded. "Meet you back at home."

His father turned around and dropped him off again at the end of the street where the suspect had disappeared between the houses and into the woods behind. Sweeping the flashlight in front of him, Ryan slowly retraced the path he'd taken a quarter hour earlier. A pity it hadn't rained in several nights; otherwise, there might be footprints to find instead of only bare, packed dirt and crispy, dehydrated grass.

His search proved fruitless. As he reached his parents' yard, the beam of his father's flashlight danced over tree trunks and bushes at the edge of the woods. After a minute, Jim turned and met him at the back deck.

"Find anything?" Ryan asked.

"Maybe." His father flicked the light along the tree line. "There's some trampled brush leading back into the woods. Maybe an animal, but I'd guess it was our man's way in." He led the way around to the garage and inside the back hallway, where Jim let a large yawn slip out of his mouth as they headed for the kitchen. "I'm getting too old for this job."

Ryan smiled as he unbuttoned his uniform shirt and took off the heavy flak jacket. He rolled his shoulders, then slipped his shirt back on. "Thanks for your help, Dad. You go back to bed. I want to talk to Laney about what happened."

She sat across from his mother at the dining table, her hands wrapped around a mug of tea. For a moment, the sight of her so at home in *his* childhood home stole the breath from his lungs.

But the dark circles beneath her eyes, her pale face and her disheveled hair reminded him painfully of what she'd been through tonight. What a close call she'd had.

Thank You, Lord, for Your protection over Laney, he prayed as he walked around the kitchen island and into the breakfast nook. He rested a hand on his mother's shoulder. She sat opposite Laney. "Hey, Mom, thanks for looking after her."

His mother glanced up at him, a twinkle in her eye. "Is that my cue to leave you two alone?" She'd certainly never left him wondering how she felt about Laney, even back before they'd started dating. Looking across the table, he noted Laney's cheeks tint pink.

"No, it just means you can go back to bed if you want to."

Mary stood. "Well, at least let me get you a cup of tea too. Or do you want a decaf?"

"Whatever's easiest. Thanks, Mom." He slid onto the chair on the end as Mary retreated into the kitchen and tinkered with the coffee maker. Anything from her kitchen would be better than the watered-down sludge they drank at the station.

"Hey," he said gently, stretching a hand across the table. Close but not touching Laney's where it still clutched her mug. "I'm sorry I couldn't stay to help. Are you okay?"

For the first time, her lips turned up into a tiny smile. "It's fine, Ryan. I knew you had to chase him. I wanted you to." She glanced past him, through the kitchen, as if looking for Jim. "I take it you didn't get him?"

"No." He ran a hand over his cheeks and chin, exhaustion settling over his shoulders. These last few days had felt endlessly long. "He had his route planned. Knew exactly where to go to keep out of the lights."

Mary reappeared from the kitchen and deposited a mug of frothy coffee with cream on the table. The smell was enough to ease the tension in his shoulders. "It's decaf hazelnut."

"Perfect." He took a sip of the hot liquid, waving goodnight to his mother as she left the room.

"Thank you, Mary," Laney added.

"Goodnight, kids," she said.

The same words she'd used all the time back when they *were* kids. He met Laney's gaze to see a hint of laughter playing on her lips, and yet she fiddled with her mug as if she was embarrassed.

He cleared his throat. "So, I've got an APB out on the suspect for tonight, and we'll send in a team at first light to double check the woods around here. Hopefully some leads will turn up."

She nodded, then stared down into her mug.

His fingers itched with the urge to take her hand, so instead, he took another sip of coffee. "Can you tell me what happened? In detail? Anything you can remember might help."

He listened as she slowly recounted how she'd been studying the case files when she remembered the unlocked door. How she'd taken a poker from the fireplace instead of waking his father. How the door had been open and the man had jumped her right here, mere feet from where he now sat.

Anger burned like fire inside his ribs, until he had to stand up. "Laney, I am so sorry. I shouldn't have gone back to the station. It was stupid to leave you here."

She shook her head wearily. "I wasn't alone, Ryan. Your parents were here. I could've woken them up if I'd truly been concerned. I just… It was stupid of me. *I'm* sorry."

Using a clean dishtowel, he picked up the fireplace poker. A scratch marred the floor's finish where it had struck the wood. Another scar to remember something awful. Why did life have to leave so many of them?

"You have nothing to be sorry for," he said, setting the poker carefully on the table. His law enforcement mind was already busy dusting it for prints, but the part of him that had never stopped caring about Laney could focus only on her. If he was being honest, his feelings for her were seeping through the wall he'd built around his heart like water through a cracked dam.

How would he stay afloat if he fell for her again?

From the way she was watching him now, eyes following his every move, maybe she still shared those feelings. Was there hope for them?

Should there be, after the way she'd left so abruptly?

But it wasn't truly her fault. *He* was the one who'd let things change. Maybe the time had finally come to try to make things right.

"Laney?" He almost lost his nerve when her brows lifted a touch and she swallowed. More open to him than she'd been in a decade. But a man had to do the right thing, especially when given another opportunity. "I need to apologize to you."

Laney knew what was coming the second the words popped out of Ryan's mouth. Maybe it was the way he rubbed the back of his neck in embarrassment or the way his eyes had softened as he looked at her. They were encroaching on dangerous territory, but she didn't have the heart to stop him.

She squirmed in her seat. "For what?"

He stared down at his hands—so much stronger now than when he'd been a teenager. Man's hands, capable of keeping her and so many others safe. "I think you know, but I'll say it anyway. For that night the week before graduation. I *never* should've let things go that far."

Heat crept up her neck and into her face, making the tips of her ears burn. "We were kids, Ryan. And that took two people."

But he shook his head, lips pressed together. "Even not being a believer, I still knew better. You deserved my respect in that area of our relationship, and you didn't get it. God, in His mercy, protected us from the big consequences, but it changed our relationship anyway. I'm sorry for that."

Her breath froze in her lungs, and she clenched a hand under the table. Now would be the right time to tell him the truth—that they almost *had* faced a life-altering consequence. That she'd come *this close* to becoming her mother. The single mom in the trailer park—though in her heart of hearts she knew Ryan would never have let her raise a child alone, even as a teenager.

But how did one drop a secret like that on their ex-boyfriend? Especially when she'd miscarried the baby before she'd even reached eight weeks?

No, she hadn't told him then, and she didn't need to tell him now. Some secrets were better left buried.

It took effort to relax her hand and reach for her mug of tea again. Only dregs were left in the bottom. She swirled them around, watching the golden liquid dance across the white ceramic. "I'm sorry too. I'm sorry all of it worked out the way it did."

"Why did you leave?" He tilted his head to one side, watching her, his gaze thoughtful. "Was it because of me?"

"No." *Liar.* She sighed. After how much he'd gone through for her in the last few days, could she really lie right to his face? "And yes. After what happened between us...and all those plans we had for the future...I got scared. I didn't want to end up alone in a trailer park."

And I couldn't face your family after I told Jenna to go out alone that day. Even now, the thought of how much the truth would hurt them... It was unbearable.

A muscle ticked in his jaw until he let out a long breath. "You know I would *never* have let that happen, don't you?"

"I know. But we don't always make the best decisions as teenagers, do we?"

"No, we don't."

She offered him a smile, waving a finger at his uniform. "You turned out the way I always imagined you would."

"Financially soluble and ruggedly handsome, with killer biceps?" He winked as he flexed an arm, revealing impressive muscles beneath his shirt sleeve.

"More or less." She laughed. "And me? Other than the short hair, am I what you imagined?"

His expression shifted, the laughter fading into something more subdued. Deeper, as if he were tapping into a connection between them that could outlast time itself. "No, Laney. You are so much more—more alive, stronger, more accomplished—"

"Or do you mean *ambitious*?" She smirked, but he

wouldn't be derailed from the serious turn of his conversation.

"More beautiful than ever. Inside and out."

Her heart skipped a beat. How could he think so highly of her after the way she had treated him?

Reality intervened before her feelings got carried away. No matter how attractive Ryan was now, no matter how many feelings still simmered between them, nothing could happen. Not with the secrets she still kept. She was heading back to the Smithsonian and her job as soon as this case was over.

"Ryan, I…"

Her expression must've said it all, because when he smiled, his eyes looked sad. "It's been a long night, Laney. You need some rest. I'm going to double check the locks on the window in your room, and then I'll sleep up here on the couch. Just in case anybody tries to break in again."

"Thank you." Truth was, she'd feel a thousand times better knowing he was close at hand. No one else had ever had the ability to make her feel as safe. Or cared for. Or loved. *Stop it*, she chided herself.

He stood, and when he offered his hand, it felt natural to let him pull her to her feet with her nose inches away from his broad chest. Closer than they'd been in a long time.

Before she could object, he wrapped both arms around her and tugged her into an embrace. She melted into his warmth and comfort, feeling as at home in his arms as she had with his mother at the dining table. Alarm bells in her head told her to step away, but surely a moment wouldn't hurt? After all, she'd been through a traumatic couple of days.

"I know you're going home soon," he said, his chin lowered to the top of her head. "And I know our lives have gone in different directions and we don't want anything to happen between us. But I'm not going to lie about how good it is to see you again, Laney."

She swallowed, pulling her head back from his chest to look up at him. "It's good to see you too." Her voice came out far weaker than it should have.

His eyes roamed her face for another second before he released her and stepped away. Her back felt suddenly cold without his arms. He tipped his head in the direction of the guest room. "Come on. Time for you to go to bed."

As she followed him down the hallway, Laney couldn't stop replaying his words in her mind. *We don't want anything to happen between us.* Neither could she help noticing the disappointment nudging at her heart at the thought he was content without her in his life.

ELEVEN

Laney blinked awake at the buzzing sound coming from the nightstand. She groped for her phone and pried open her sleepy eyes to find a text from the Smithsonian. The package containing the remains had arrived. Her colleagues said they'd dive into the analysis right away.

She flopped onto her back, groaning in pain as her muscles protested. Apparently that struggle last night had cost her more effort than she'd realized. Her throat was tender and bruised, too, from the assailant's arm wrapped around her neck. A constant reminder that if they didn't catch him soon, she might experience far worse. Shuddering, she glanced at the time on her phone and jerked upright.

It was nearly 8:00 a.m. Ryan had let her sleep way too long, considering the way this case kept growing out of control, like a tumor. She flung back the covers and threw on some clothes—the same too-long blue jeans and black shirt as yesterday, thanks to her limited wardrobe. Somehow, heading to a department store to shop didn't feel important at the moment.

After brushing her teeth in the guest bathroom and running a comb through her unruly hair, she grabbed her laptop and headed out to the living room. The couch was empty, but a pile of messy blankets indicated Ryan had been sleeping there not too long before.

"Hey, sleepyhead." He stood in the kitchen, holding a coffee cup and leaning against the island, one long leg casually crossed over the other. Instead of his uniform, he wore a pair of blue jeans and a dark gray CrossFit T-shirt that complemented his dark eyes…and explained where all those muscles had come from. Maybe she'd been staring a little too long, because he added, "Technically it's my day off. But I figured you wouldn't want to relax around here all day."

"No, not after last night." Her voice came out a bit too high. Must be time for coffee. She snatched a mug from the cabinet and made a beeline for the Keurig on the opposite counter. Selecting a K-Cup from the rack bought her a few precious moments to compose herself. It wasn't the memory of last night's attack that was so unsettling— it was thinking about being wrapped up in Ryan's arms. There was no doubt they'd reconnected and bridged one of the gaps between them, but she hadn't expected it to affect her this way. Like an open door for all the old emotions.

"How are you feeling?" He didn't move, but she could almost imagine the warmth and strength emanating from him if he walked over to her.

Foolish thoughts. She rolled her shoulders. "Stiff, but I slept well." After starting the coffee maker, she faced him and leaned against the counter, nearly mimicking his pose. "I might have a bit of bruising on my trachea too. For a moment there last night, I thought he might strangle me."

Ryan pushed away from the kitchen island without a moment's hesitation and crossed the gap between them. Warm fingers lifted her chin, tilting her face one way and then the other as he inspected her neck. His jaw muscles tightened, and when he released her, his eyes burned. "We need to have a doctor examine you. To document the evidence."

"Sure, if you think it'll come up in court." When the coffee maker clicked off, she took the steaming cup and stirred in sugar. "There's something I need to go over with you about the Wilson case anyway. I'd like to see the transcripts of the trial."

"Not without breakfast, you two," Mary called from the table. "I've got cold cereal and yogurt out here, or you can toast a bagel."

The curtains in the breakfast nook were back to their usual innocuous arrangement, tied off on either end of the sliding door. Only the pair of police officers down at the tree line indicated anything out of the ordinary had happened.

At Laney's questioning glance, Ryan explained, "They got here an hour ago. We processed the inside first—" he waved an arm around the breakfast area "—but didn't find anything. Now they're out back with my father, trying to retrace the route the man took to get into the yard. We'll analyze the fireplace poker just in case the assailant left prints."

After a quick bowl of cereal and a visit to a physician's office, Ryan drove them back to the police station.

"It's starting to feel like a second home in here," Laney joked as she followed him to his desk. She could even greet the other officers by name.

"Don't get too attached. We don't have the budget to hire a forensic anthropologist of your caliber." The twinkle in his eye suggested he was joking, and yet Laney couldn't help wondering if deep down he *wanted* her to go back to DC. Were those feelings from last night all in her head?

She laughed it off anyway, because it was better this way. They'd agreed nothing would happen between them for a reason. Before Ryan could grab a chair for her, she helped herself, rolling it over to his desk.

He turned on the computer and clicked through a series of screens to pull up the file she wanted. "The transcripts from the Wilson trial… Here you go. This document is hundreds of pages long, though. What are you looking for, exactly?"

"You said Wilson insisted on his innocence, right?"

"Yeah. He pleaded not guilty."

"Did the possibility of him being framed come up in the trial?"

Ryan's eyes narrowed. "You found something, didn't you? Spill."

She laid her laptop on the desk, opening to the key photographs she'd sorted last night. "Here are pictures of the inferior or lower end of the right femur of each victim. The killer used some implement—presumably the knife from Wilson's kitchen—to separate the leg above the patella." She inhaled a slow breath, tapping the gallery app on her phone. Waiting to see Ryan's reaction. "Here's a picture I took yesterday morning. From Jenna's remains."

He glanced back and forth between the phone and the laptop screen, the color slowly siphoning out of his face. "They're the same."

"Yes." She held up her hand. "There are a couple of possibilities here, though. One is that our soft identification of the remains from the bog as Jenna isn't correct. They could still be your other cold case from a year later, making this one of Wilson's victims. Alternatively…"

"Wilson was framed, and there's a serial killer on the loose." He rubbed both hands over his face, then leaned back in his chair, staring at the corkboard over his desk. Jenna smiled back at them, her face just as Laney remembered.

"I want to know if Wilson accused anyone else in the trial. Maybe when he was on the stand. Did he claim anyone specific was framing him?" She pointed at the monitor. "Can you search the transcript?"

The keyboard clacked beneath his fingers as he typed into the search field. Together they scanned the highlighted passages in silence, looking for anything useful.

Nothing. When his defense attorney had tried to guide Wilson into explaining how he'd been set up, the prosecutor objected. *Question lacks foundation. Speculation.* The judge had agreed. No names were given.

"Let's try the lawyer," she said. "He'd know what Wilson intended to say."

It took a minute for Ryan to find the firm's phone number and place the call. He put the phone on speaker so she could hear. An office assistant answered and let them know the attorney wasn't available at the moment. Ryan left a message.

"Hopefully he'll get back to us ASAP."

Laney sucked the inside of her lip. "What about Wilson? He's at Indiana State Prison, right? Can we get an interview?"

Ryan balled his hand into a fist and tapped it gently on the desktop. "Wilson's dead. I never got the chance to tell you, but I spoke to the warden last night. He was killed in the yard two months ago."

"How convenient." She pressed her lips together.

"You're thinking the killer is behind his death too?"

She shrugged. "It's all conjecture. But you said it's been two years since the last disappearance here. Maybe after framing Wilson, your serial killer planned on ending his spree. Only now he's realized he can't stop, and he wanted to shut Wilson up permanently beforehand."

"There's definitely a motive. It'd have to be someone who knew Wilson."

"Makes sense, given they 'borrowed' one of his kitchen knives a few different times." She wrinkled her nose.

Ryan nodded. "Okay, I can see that. I'll contact the prison again to get a list of anyone who had contact with Wilson from the outside. Maybe the killer kept tabs on him. We can also dig for information on his personal life from before the trial."

Without waiting for a response, he picked up the phone again and tapped out a number, then pressed the receiver to his ear. She only half listened as he asked for the warden and was placed on hold.

None of this explained why the killer was still targeting *her*. Sure, they wanted to cover their tracks and avoid being identified, but the remains were already en route to the Smithsonian. There wasn't any reason to go after her now.

Unless…there was more to Jenna's original disappearance than she knew. Jenna had been her best friend. They were almost always together. If Jenna's death was premeditated, had Laney been a target too? Was the killer hoping to finish the job?

Such a horrible thought. A shiver worked its way up her back until Ryan took one of her hands into his.

Not appropriate for colleagues, and yet…they'd never just be colleagues, would they?

Friends—it was appropriate for friends.

He squeezed her hand and let go as someone came on the other end of the line. "Yes, this is Sergeant Mitchell again. I'm looking for a list of visitors, known friends and family, or contacts for Ronald Wilson." A pause, then Ryan nodded. "Okay, thanks. I'd appreciate that."

"Well?" she asked as soon as he hung up.

"He's going to pull together what they have and send it to me."

"All right."

"Hey, Mitchell," one of the other officers called from his desk, "Mike Roberts up in Indy sent word your suspects checked out clean. No trace of explosives. Meant to tell you when you got here."

"Thanks, Ross." He turned to Laney. "Dad got us the warrant to search Dennis Taber's house. Sarah's taking Marty over there later this morning. I figured we should lie low and give you time to recover, but…" His voice trailed away, one eyebrow lifting. Very much like the expression that had lit up his face as a teenager whenever one of their friends suggested they sneak into the fields for a midnight game of tag.

Ryan always knew exactly where and when to push. She'd never been one to back down from a challenge, so she gave the same answer she always had. "Let's do it. Especially since I now have a very personal reference to the suspect's height and weight."

Her last comment brought a frown to his face, and for a moment she wondered if he'd change his mind. Decide it wasn't safe enough. But with the possibility of a serial killer after her, where *was* she going to be safe?

Maybe the same thoughts were playing through Ryan's mind, because after they stood, he wrapped an arm around her shoulders. "I suppose offense is the best defense. But you're sticking close to me, okay?"

"Got it." She couldn't imagine she'd feel safer anywhere else.

Unlike their visit to Lawrence Brown's house, Dennis Taber opened the door after the first knock. Ryan recognized him immediately, despite the graininess of the airport's surveillance footage. He held up his badge and the search warrant.

"Dennis Taber, I'm Sergeant Ryan Mitchell. We have a warrant to search your property with the dog—" he nodded toward the German shepherd, held tightly on the leash by Sarah "—and ask you some questions."

Dennis's brow furrowed. "What for? What am I accused of?"

"You're not accused of anything yet, sir. We're investigating a bombing that may be related to the airport. Your cooperation will help us get to the bottom of what happened."

The tall man swung the door open. "Of course, I'll cooperate. If this is about what happened at that hotel, I didn't have anything to do with it." He stepped aside as Sarah led Marty in.

Marty stopped in front of Dennis, sniffing his shoes and pant legs. Then the dog strained at the leash, telling Sarah to let him keep going into the house.

Ryan exchanged a quick glance with Laney before turning back to Dennis. Looked like the man was clean, but maybe something could still turn up in the house. "We've got some questions for you. Would you prefer to do that at the police station, or are you willing to cooperate here?"

"I'll answer your questions."

"Excellent." He pulled out a notepad and pen. Laney stood close beside him on the front porch. "Mr. Taber, we have on record that you and Lawrence Brown unloaded Flight 776 from Indianapolis on the evening of August 17. Is that correct?"

Dennis scratched his head. "Uh, yeah, sounds right. I mean, I was working that night, so it would've been me and Larry."

"Do you recall anything unusual happening with the luggage from that flight?"

"No." He stared over their shoulders for a moment, thinking. "Wait—yes. Larry said we missed a bag. I was the one who drove the truck up to the claim belt. We each unloaded a side, and when we were done, I returned the truck. When I got back to our workstation fifteen minutes later, Larry said he'd found one we overlooked putting on the belt. I offered to take it up to the claims office, but he said he'd take care of it."

"How does the unloading work? Does the luggage go directly from the truck onto the conveyor?"

"It's less work to throw them right on the belt than to unload to the floor, but sometimes one topples back if it's not balanced. Or they can fall off the truck while you're grabbing another. We miss one every now and then."

"Did you see the bag in question?"

"It was a black carry-on." He held his hands up to indicate the approximate size. "You know, one of those small rolling ones. Larry found it by the belt and left it against the wall in the baggage handlers' work area. Same place we always leave missing luggage before taking it upstairs."

Great. How many other employees had access to Laney's suitcase during that time? Maybe they'd find video surveillance for that area, too, if they kept watching the footage.

"Why didn't he just put it on the conveyor?"

"Policy says take it to the claims office if the belt's been off more than fifteen minutes."

"Was it ever left unattended?" Ryan asked.

"Dunno." Dennis shrugged. "I mean, I wasn't there, because I was driving the truck back. You'd have to ask Larry."

Ryan glanced at Laney, wondering if he'd missed any other questions she wanted him to ask.

She cleared her throat. "Other than when you returned the truck, was Lawrence Brown with you the entire time you were unloading?"

"Yeah. Why wouldn't he be? We had a job to do."

"Okay, thank you, Mr. Taber," Ryan said. "We'll let you know if we have any further questions."

Sarah and Marty reappeared in the entryway behind Dennis. She shook her head ever so slightly. Nothing. Ryan clenched his teeth as frustration ripped at his insides. Laney's life was in danger, and if they didn't get a lead soon… Would he be able to protect her the next time?

"All right, all finished," Sarah said lightly. "Thanks so much, Mr. Taber. We appreciate your cooperation."

"Of course," he said, letting Sarah and Marty back out of the house.

"Please let us know if you remember anything else that might be helpful," Ryan added.

Dennis closed the door and the three headed for the patrol cars in the driveway.

Ryan stopped next to Sarah as she loaded the dog back into his crate. "Really? Nothing at all?"

"Nothing," she said. "I'm not sure his scent was even

on the bag from incidental handling, but of course, a blast like that obliterates most smells beyond charcoal."

Ryan returned to his car, where Laney already sat in the passenger seat, and slid in behind the wheel. "What did you think about him?"

"Too tall for last night's attacker. The man who grabbed me was shorter than you by at least a couple of inches—closer to Lawrence Brown's height—and this guy was easily six foot four."

Did she always gauge other men's heights relative to his? It took effort not to smile.

"Besides," she added, "my instincts say to believe him."

This time he did smile. "We'll make a decent cop out of you yet, you know it? I agree, though. He seems clean. But then, Brown came back clean, too, according to the dog."

"And there's no way Brown had time to come threaten me in the bathroom in the middle of unloading the airplane. The timing doesn't work." She let out a slight sigh. "Now what?"

"Well—" He was interrupted by the crackling static of the radio.

"Two-one-five. Ten-thirty-three. Copy?"

Ryan spoke into his radio. "Ten-four. Mitchell here."

"We've got a ten-twenty on an abandoned blue Ford pickup."

He exchanged a quick glance with Laney. Her eyes had gone wide in that "what are we waiting for?" expression he'd always loved. Finally, maybe they would get some answers.

TWELVE

Laney frowned out the window as they headed away from town on one of the many country roads. Here was yet another familiar path she and Jenna had biked during that last year together. Like the road to Lawrence Brown's house, the scenery was hauntingly familiar but foreign at the same time, as if she'd seen it all before but had never really been paying attention.

She picked at her fingernails as they rounded a bend. This could've been the same road Jenna was on that fatal day. Come to think of it, the area did look familiar. Up ahead at the next curve, two cop cars were pulled over on the right-hand shoulder. A hill rose on the left side of the road, and to the right, on the other side of a guardrail, the terrain dropped away out of sight.

Ryan slowed the vehicle, pulling in behind the other cars. "Here?" He said it more like a question than a statement.

At his expression, dread curled in her stomach. "This is where they found Jenna's bike, isn't it?"

He turned off the engine and stared at the guardrail.

An entire section of the metal had broken free from its support on one end and now lay twisted and mangled beside the road. Hit by the truck, perhaps?

When he finally turned to her, the grief in his eyes said it all.

Anger boiled Laney's insides. This had to be an intentional choice by the killer—someone who knew Jenna's father and brother worked for the police. Someone sadistic enough to play with them, torture them over their loss.

She squeezed Ryan's arm, offering him the only measure of comfort she could. "I'm sorry, Ryan. We'll catch him."

A muscle twitched in his jaw. "We don't even have a legitimate suspect yet."

"We'll get there, though. Justice is in the Lord's hands. He won't leave evildoers unpunished forever."

His gaze met hers, and he gave her a small smile. "You're right. Thanks, Laney. I don't know how I'd get through this without you."

Ryan's words filled her insides with a different sort of warmth than the fierce, burning anger. For the first time since she'd returned, she let her gaze drift to his mouth, remembering what his kiss had felt like. Would it be the same now, so many years later? From that tender look in his eyes, he might very well be asking himself the same question.

Tension crackled between them until he cleared his throat.

Right. The case.

And friends *only*. Wasn't that their unspoken agreement?

She bolted out of the car like it was on fire, sucking in a couple of deep breaths as she waited for Ryan. He didn't make eye contact as he rounded the front of the vehicle and examined the damaged guardrail. On the opposite side, a set of ruts in the grass showed where the truck had braked on the other side before sliding down the hill. It had come to rest a hundred feet below, against a tree.

Two officers stood beside the open driver's door. A third climbed out of the front patrol car as she and Ryan approached.

"Sergeant," the officer said in greeting.

"What have you got so far?" Ryan asked.

"Ford F-150, 1993 for the year. VIN currently unregistered. Previous registration was in Indiana, under one Ted Kincaide, expired six months ago. Plates are missing from the exterior, but we waited for you to arrive before processing the interior."

"Who found it? You can't see it from the road unless you pull off on the shoulder up there."

"An anonymous man called it in. Said he pulled over to let another car pass and happened to notice it."

"All right," Ryan said. "Then let's get started."

Laney helped him carry down the evidence-collection kit from the patrol car, while the other officer used a digital camera to photograph the broken guardrail and the ruts in the ground. Judging by the scraped bark on a couple of the trees she passed, the truck had ricocheted off more than one on its descent.

The inside was disgusting—full of old McDonald's wrappers, rotting chicken nuggets, drinking straws and scratched-off, expired lottery tickets. Laney donned a pair of gloves and dug in, assisting Ryan with bagging and labeling each item he pulled from the truck's extended cab back seat.

"Plenty of material for DNA analysis," she said with a wrinkled nose.

"Absolutely." An officer working on the front seat held up a pair of tweezers, a nearly invisible hair glinting in the sunlight. "Though there might be *too* much here to be helpful."

"Hey, here're the plates." Ryan pivoted on the edge of the truck and held up a pair of Indiana license tags. He jumped down off the running board. "I'll take these up to the patrol car and run them through the system." He glanced at her. "You coming, Laney?"

"Sure. I'll call the hospital to check on my mom while we're up there." With the help of the social worker, Kim had yielded to Laney's wishes and agreed to check herself into a rehab center as soon as she was released from the hospital.

She trudged back up the hillside next to him in silence. Thick gray clouds had appeared over the rise and now obscured the sun, giving the place an even gloomier feel than it had before. The hot, muggy air threatened a doozy of a thunderstorm later.

Her cell phone was in her purse inside the patrol car, so while Ryan sat in the driver's seat and typed the plate number into his onboard computer, she grabbed the bag and walked to the rear of the vehicle. As she pulled her phone out of its slot, a folded piece of paper fluttered to the ground.

Probably a receipt. She really needed to clean out that bag. After finding the hospital's number, she tapped it in and went through the menu until she could enter her mother's room number. While it rang, she stooped to pick up the piece of paper.

Huh. Ripped edges, like it had been torn from something larger. The outside was white, but a glimpse of color stared back at her from inside.

"Hello?" Her mother's voice came on the phone.

"Hi, Mom, I just wanted to check on you," Laney answered, only half concentrating as she opened the folded piece of paper.

It was part of a map. And on top of the red roads and green fields, scrawled black words sent a cold chill threading through her veins.

It'll be your turn soon, Laney Hamilton.

Ryan finished reading the report he'd pulled up on the license plate number, which essentially confirmed what they'd learned from the VIN. Ted Kincaide was the last registered owner, but the plates had expired six months ago.

"Looks like we need to pay a visit to Ted Kincaide," he said as he climbed out of the car. Laney sat in silence on the rear bumper, her back to him, staring down at something. Had she gotten bad news?

"Hey," he said as he walked up to her. "Is your mother okay?"

She glanced up and her hands trembled as she held out a piece of paper. His throat closed as he read the threat, fear and anger fighting for the same space in his chest.

"Where did you get this?" he asked.

"It was in my purse." Her words were faint. She reached a thumb over her shoulder. "There, in the car."

"Are you sure it wasn't there earlier?"

"I'm sure. That pocket was empty when I put my phone in it this morning."

He scanned the road, the hill on the opposite side and the bend up ahead. No sign of any cars or people, except for the three officers down the hill. Could the killer have been so bold? Sneaking into his car to leave this message? And why?

"He's playing with us, Ryan." She muttered the words

mechanically, still staring at her hands. "Just like leaving the truck here where you found the bike. He's probably the one who called in the location."

He shook his head. "He already tried and failed to abduct you. This is only a scare tactic. We must be getting close to identifying him." She stood, and he slipped his arm around her shoulder and pulled her close almost without thinking. "I'm going to protect you."

"I know." The words came out like a sigh, as if she wanted to believe him but didn't really.

Frustration gnawed at his insides as he wished for some way to reassure her, to make things right. She squirmed a little and he let go.

"Can I see that paper again?" she asked.

He handed it back to her, hating its very existence and that she'd ever gotten involved in this case.

She tapped the paper. "Look, this was ripped off the edge of a city map. Here's the far east end of Sandy Bluff and County Highway 13, heading east. The trailer park's up here." She pointed out the various landmarks beneath the ugly black words. "The field where you found the other two bodies. And Waltman's Bog."

Her finger stopped over the bog, hovering for a moment. Ryan leaned closer, squinting. Was that a mark on the map? No, make that *two* marks. He glanced up at Laney, his eyes growing wide. "Are you thinking what I'm thinking?"

"He's given us the location of another set of remains. But why?" Her brows pulled together. "Why tell us this after going to such lengths to silence me? Is it a trap?"

Ryan clenched his jaw as he stared at the paper. "I don't know." He hated having to give her that answer but lying would never work. Not with Laney, who'd always been able to read the truth right off his face.

She held out the scrap. "What do we do about this?"

Good question. Taking Laney into that bog to search for remains was the last thing he wanted to do if it was a trap. But if the remains were there, they needed those bones. The other victim's family deserved to know what had happened to their daughter, just like his family wanted to know about Jenna.

"I'll talk to my father about it," he said after a long moment, tucking the map into the back pocket of his jeans. "In the meantime, let's pay a visit to the former owner of that truck." He pointed down the hill to where the officers were still at work on the vehicle. "I'll call Sarah to see if she and Marty can meet us over there."

First stop was another visit to the judge for a warrant. She barely batted an eyelash at yet another request. "I hope you find him this time," she said.

"Me too."

Back in the car, Ryan plugged Ted Kincaide's address into his GPS and drove with Laney south of town, past Sandy Bluff's equivalent of an industrial zone. Large flat-roofed warehouses and abandoned factories whizzed by as he followed the highway toward the farm fields beyond the city outskirts. A couple of lower-end neighborhoods sprawled out here—cheap construction, cookie-cutter design and only the tiny trees the builder had planted after razing anything worth keeping.

He stopped in front of Kincaide's house and let the car idle as they waited for Sarah. The driveway of the yellow split-level home was empty and the double-garage door was closed, giving no indication whether the owner was home.

"What does Kincaide do for a living?" Laney asked. "Would he have been able to plant the bomb in my suitcase?"

"That's a good question. Lawrence Brown certainly had better opportunity. But based on the size difference between the airport-bathroom attacker and the man from last night, we're looking for two people. Maybe he had help."

Sarah drove up in her SUV and pulled into the driveway. Ryan and Laney got out to meet her, in what was starting to feel like a daily addition to his routine.

She pointed at his jeans and T-shirt, now topped by a heavy flak jacket he'd brought from the station. "Nice day off, Mitchell."

He shrugged. "Too bad we don't get overtime." But even though they made light of it, truth was, protecting Laney was his top priority. And that meant catching this killer as soon as possible.

He knocked on the front door and had to bite back his surprise when a brown-haired man answered. Didn't anyone in this town have a day job?

Beside him, Laney stiffened ever so slightly. He glanced between her and the man, noting he was close to the height and build of last night's attacker. But unfortunately that description would fit a quarter of the population of Sandy Bluff.

"Ted Kincaide?" he asked. When the man nodded, he showed the warrant and ran through his speech about searching the premises with the dog.

Kincaide's face paled, but he stepped aside to allow Sarah and Marty inside. "What's this about?"

"Do you own a blue Ford F-150 truck, extended cab?" Ryan asked.

The man's Adam's apple bobbed, and his gaze flicked nervously between Ryan and the police cars parked on the street and in his driveway. Clearly he had something to hide. Did they have their suspect?

"I used to," he said, shifting his weight from one leg to the other. "But not anymore."

"What happened to it? Did you sell it?"

He slowly shook his head. "It was stolen. A while ago."

Something about his evasive answer wasn't adding up. If anyone had reported that truck missing, it would've been flagged when Ryan searched the system. "Why didn't you report it?"

"I…" Kincaide glanced into the house. Wiped his palms on his jeans.

Ryan shifted to the right, positioning himself between Kincaide and Laney. The man had hardly given her a second glance, but his nervous behavior made him unpredictable.

Just then his radio crackled. *"Two-one-five, ten-sixty-eight in the garage."* Sarah's voice. She had found something. *"Ten-twenty-six. Copy?"*

For a second Kincaide's wide eyes met Ryan's, and terror flicked across his features. Then desperation.

Ryan flung an arm backward to push Laney behind him at the same moment Kincaide pulled a handgun.

He aimed it straight at Ryan's face.

THIRTEEN

Ryan's hand immediately went to the gun holstered in his waistband.

"Don't move," Kincaide muttered through gritted teeth. "I don't know what she found, but I didn't do anything wrong."

"You're holding an officer at gunpoint, Mr. Kincaide. That's a felony in Indiana."

Kincaide swiped his palm against his pants again. "I don't want to, Sergeant. But I'm not going to jail for something I didn't do."

He sensed Laney shifting behind him before she spoke. "What didn't you do, Ted?"

The man's brows pulled together. "Who is she? Is she a police officer too? What do you want with me?"

"Why don't you lower the gun, and we'll talk about it?" Ryan said soothingly.

The gun wavered, but Kincaide clapped his other hand over the trembling first one. "Not till you tell me what I'm accused of."

With a loud whir, the garage door rolled open. Kincaide started at the sudden noise, the gun bobbling again as he stepped out onto the sidewalk. Ryan seized his chance, taking advantage of the distraction to twist the weapon out of the man's grasp. A second later and he had the cuffs out, securing Kincaide's hands behind his back.

"We'll have to discuss it down at the station, because you're under arrest."

"Officer McIntosh, what did you find?" Laney asked as they followed the sidewalk back to the driveway.

Ryan pushed Kincaide in front of him until they reached the open garage. A single car stood on the left side of the stall.

Sarah was in the back, where metal shelves stood against the wall connected with the house. "Marty alerted here," she said, pointing to a pile of rags stuffed between two of the shelving units. Protruding from the top of the pile were a couple of metal pipes. From beneath, the corner of a bag jutted out. Sarah toed some of the rags aside to read the bag's label. *Ammonium nitrate fertilizer.* "Components for a pipe bomb."

"Those aren't mine!" Kincaide insisted. "I have no idea how they got here."

"Bag them," Ryan said, ignoring him. "Call for backup if you need it. I'm taking this one to lockup. Laney…" He broke away, undecided for a moment. Taking her in the car with a potential killer ran against all his instincts but letting her leave his care wasn't appealing either.

"I'll ride back with Officer McIntosh," she said. At his look, she added, "I'll be *fine*, Ryan."

Laney let out a long breath as she watched Ryan stuff Ted Kincaide into the back of his patrol car. The man clearly had something to hide, but was he serial-killer material? Somehow she doubted it.

But he had substances for explosives right here in the garage... Could he be the accomplice?

She glanced at Sarah. "Want me to get the evidence bags from the car?"

"That'd be great." The other woman patted her dog, saying softly, "Good boy, Marty. You get extra treats tonight."

When Laney returned to the garage, Sarah had already pulled out the materials in question. Laney threw on a pair of gloves and helped record and bag the rags and containers.

As they worked, Sarah said, "So...it's totally not my business—" she flashed Laney a smile "—but what's going on between you and Mitchell?"

Heat crept into her cheeks. Was the attraction she kept fighting so obvious to everyone? "We're old friends."

"Friends?" Sarah arched one of her blond eyebrows.

"All right, we used to date in high school." Even though Sarah appeared close to her age, Laney didn't remember her from school. Why was she telling her this? Probably because the woman managed to seem both kind and trustworthy at the same time, and Laney had no one else to confide in. Maybe it was the uniform. "I take it you didn't grow up here."

"No, I lived with my mom up the road in Jasper. Moved back here because of some family stuff. Anyway, rumors were flying around the department after Chief Mitchell called you, but I didn't pay attention to them. People like to gossip, you know? Especially in a small town. But—" she shot Laney a conspiratorial look "—now that I've seen you two together, I'm inclined to believe them."

"Well, it doesn't matter, because I'm heading home in a few days. As soon as we wrap up this case." Laney finished labeling the exterior of the bag she'd just sealed.

Sarah stood and began placing the bags into a plastic bin. "Hopefully this evidence will be what you need."

"I hope so." Laney added hers to the collection.

"It's a shame, though," Sarah said as she and Laney carried the bin to the SUV. Marty trotted along behind them on his leash. "Mitchell's a great guy. Team player, smart, considerate, always has your back. His family's been through the wringer."

Laney paused at the back of the SUV, propping the bin on her knee as Sarah lifted the hatchback. "If I didn't know better, I'd say *you* had a thing for him."

"Oh, no." Sarah flashed her left hand, where a large, shiny diamond sparkled on her fourth finger. "I mean, I did once. We even went out on a date, but we weren't meant for each other. Then I met Rick…" Her eyes went dreamy for a moment, and Laney had to cough to cover up how she nearly choked. It was like being trapped in a romance movie. Did people actually get to live out that kind of perpetual happiness?

When she quit coughing, Sarah added, "Anyway, it's pretty clear to me he's only ever had eyes for one woman. Just sayin'."

"Umm, thanks. I guess?" Laney wedged the bin into the back of the SUV next to Marty's crate, then climbed into the front seat to wait while Sarah loaded the dog. She'd have to be more careful how she acted around Ryan at the station. Come to think of it, she needed to be more careful how she acted around him *everywhere*. It was far too easy to slip back into couple mode with him.

A picture flew into her mind of cuddling next to him on a couch—maybe the one in her apartment back home—watching a scary movie and eating popcorn, their fingers brushing against each other in the bowl.

The thought seemed glorious and terrifying at the same time, and she was relieved when Sarah slid in behind the wheel and cranked the engine.

By the time she and Sarah reached police headquarters, Ryan was already closeted in an interrogation room with Ted Kincaide. Laney slipped into the viewing room and joined Chief Mitchell and the technician to watch the proceedings.

"Has he confessed to anything?" she asked Jim.

"No. He claims he never reported the stolen truck because he'd been driving it illegally, without renewing the plates, and didn't want to get caught. And he insists the bomb materials were planted."

She crinkled her brow. "By whom?"

Jim gestured toward the one-way window. Kincaide sat with cuffed hands on the metal tabletop, and Ryan paced back and forth opposite him.

"Okay, let's get this straight." Ryan stopped, braced both hands on the table and stared at Kincaide with a fierce expression Laney was glad she'd never been on the receiving end of. "You didn't put those chemicals in your garage? Or make any homemade explosives?"

"Please, you gotta believe me," Kincaide whined. "I failed chemistry class in high school. I don't know the first thing about bombs. And I didn't steal my own truck neither."

"Then who do you think *did* do it?"

"My ex-wife's brother. That man is scary." His eyes rounded as if to emphasize his point. "And Kathleen is obsessed with taking care of him. It's one reason we split. You heard of helicopter parents? She's a helicopter sister. I mean, I get it that they were abused as kids and all and she had to protect him growing up, but come on. He's an adult. She's gotta let him live his own life."

Ryan made a show of jotting notes down on a notepad, but it wasn't necessary. The technician was already busy pulling up marriage and divorce records for Ted Kincaide. "What's the brother's name?"

"Brown. Lawrence Brown."

Laney's insides went cold. On the other side of the two-way mirror, Ryan stiffened—subtle, but noticeable to her.

"Let's take a breather, Mr. Kincaide," he said. "I'll be back in a couple of minutes."

A moment later, Ryan stepped into the back room and leaned against the closed door, his gaze meeting Laney's. "I knew it. I *knew* Brown was involved." He balled one of his hands into a fist. "What else do we have on Kincaide?"

"Ted Kincaide has been married twice," the tech answered. "Once to Heather Morris in 1997. They divorced after eight years. He married Kathleen Brown in 2013. The divorce was filed in 2017." She tapped away at the keys for a minute. "Kathleen has a brother named Lawrence."

Ryan nodded, then glanced at Laney. "What did you guys find in the garage?"

Laney rattled off the list of components. "The fertilizer bag was nearly empty."

"It's got to be Brown. Maybe the sister is the one helping him."

Jim Mitchell held up a hand. "Hold on, Sergeant. This man might be trying to shift the blame onto someone else. You've got to follow *all* the evidence, not just whatever confirms your own suspicions. Do things by the book, got it?"

Clapping his father on the arm, he said, "Of course, Chief. I will." He pointed at Ted Kincaide. "You can deal with him."

Laney followed him out of the room and back to his desk. She pulled up a rolling chair as he sat, placing both hands on top of his head and staring at the corkboard where the victims' pictures hung.

"So someone, possibly Kathleen Kincaide or Lawrence Brown, stole Kincaide's truck and planted the bomb evidence."

Ryan nodded. "Unless Kincaide is lying…but I'm inclined to believe him."

"And that leaves the sister as a potential accomplice, maybe the one who threatened me at the airport. Unless Kincaide is the accomplice?"

"Kathleen makes more sense, if we believe her overprotective nature. Her brother turned serial killer, so she framed Ronald Wilson. When the one set of remains was discovered that could prove Wilson innocent, she panicked and threatened you. You didn't leave, so she had Lawrence plant the bomb in your suitcase and then try to abduct you."

"Okay, that makes sense. But then why are they *still* after me? We already have the remains. We know Wilson was framed. Why not pick up and run?"

Ryan didn't answer for a long moment. When he turned back to her, worry crinkled his forehead. "Laney, is there any other connection you could have to Brown? Anything else you remember about Jenna's disappearance? There's got to be something else we're missing."

"A reason he wants me for his next victim." She

pressed clammy fingers to her throat, drawing in a slow breath. "What about his history with my mother? Maybe he blames me for the break-up or wants revenge on her."

"And when he recognized your name at the airport, he saw his chance?"

She nodded, but it felt...flimsy. "I suppose. But ten years later? And why a bomb? *How* a bomb, with no previous warning?" The alternative—that she'd been his intended victim that day he'd killed Jenna—she couldn't say out loud. Not unless she was willing to discuss why Jenna had gone out alone. A shiver tickled down her spine.

"Yeah, that doesn't make much sense." Ryan squeezed her hand, pain edging his dark eyes. "Do you want to go back to your lab? I mean, wouldn't it be easier for you to help from there? It'd certainly be safer."

She shook her head. Pointed at the pictures on the corkboard, at Jenna's lovely white smile. "I'm going to see this through to the end. For them. Besides, I'm safer here with you than alone there, where he could track me down."

"All right." He pressed his lips together but nodded, and her heart lightened at the way the pain had vanished from his eyes. Instead, she found respect reflecting in them. And something else, something very much like happiness.

Once again, she found herself wishing she could turn back the clock and start again with him, to go back to those days when life was simple and all that mattered was the next math test and what they would do over the weekend.

A smile played on his lips, and his eyes crinkled. "What? Why are you looking at me like that?"

"Like what?"

"I don't know. Like it's homecoming and you're waiting for me to ask you to the dance."

"Don't be ridiculous." She straightened in her chair, suddenly fascinated by her fingernails. "That wasn't at all what I... We have work to do. What's next?"

"Today?" He glanced at the clock on the wall, which read nearly half past four o'clock. Where had the day gone? "We head to the Dairy Queen."

"Why? Does Kathleen Kincaide work there?"

"No. Because I want a Peanut Buster Parfait, and it's my day off." He winked at her, setting off a little flurry of butterflies in her stomach. Somehow his boyish charm had matured right along with him, and she found him just as attractive as ever. No, even more so.

Probably she should try to keep things neutral and ask to go back to his parents' house. But friends got ice cream together, didn't they?

Ryan couldn't stop stealing glances at Laney as they sat across from each other at a picnic table outside the Dairy Queen. She seemed to grow more beautiful every day she was here, and from the wistful way she'd been watching him earlier, she shared his sense of attraction.

Lord, what's the plan here? Why was she back in his life if she was only going to leave? Would she ever consider staying? Or...he'd stayed here to be near his parents, but enough years had passed since Jenna's death, he *could* move. Get a job out in DC.

But more importantly, if he could somehow convince her to give him a chance, would he *want* her to?

The answer to that question was pretty obvious, given the way his heart flipped every time he made eye contact with her. She smiled over a spoonful of Butterfinger Blizzard, her short hair sticking out at odd angles like a dark-haired Meg Ryan. The haircut suited her, highlighting her lovely cheekbones and wide eyes. He'd decided they were soulmates back in seventh grade, long before he'd worked up the guts to ask her out. Apparently that meant he was willing to forgive her for leaving.

But another heartbreak could easily be waiting around the bend if she stuck to her guns and went home without even considering the possibilities.

"Laney…" he started. Then stopped. Wouldn't bringing up the possibility of a relationship wreck the sort-of friendship they had going? Nearby, a table full of teen girls talked and giggled. "How's the ice cream?" he finished lamely.

"Tasty as ever. I guess some things don't change."

Did she *only* mean the ice cream?

Before he could come up with a subtle way to ask, her cell phone buzzed. She dug it out of her purse and stared at the screen for a moment, her face falling. When she looked back up at him, he didn't need to hear her words to know what she was going to say.

"Ryan—" her voice dropped. "I'm so sorry. They confirmed the identity. It's Jenna."

Probably it should've hit him harder, like a blow to the stomach that knocks out all your breath. But that space inside had been empty and hollow for so long, he only felt relieved to finally know the truth.

Talking about it was surprisingly difficult, though. "And the cause of death?"

"Blunt force trauma to the back of the skull."

He swallowed the hard knot in his throat. "Can they tell what weapon was used?"

Laney stared at her screen again for a moment before holding up a picture. The back of a skull—*Jenna's* skull—showing tiny cracks radiating out of a central fissure. Her voice wobbled when she spoke. "From the damage pattern, it appears to have been an irregularly shaped item. A rock, maybe."

"Could she have been thrown from the bike? Maybe hit by a car and then struck her head on a rock?" Maybe it hadn't been intentional. Maybe those last moments for her had passed swiftly, and she was already gone by the time the killer found her.

Laney's face crumpled like she was ready to cry any second, but she drew in a long, slow breath as she shook her head. "She was wearing a helmet, Ryan. We always wore helmets. She might've stopped for any number of reasons, but my guess is, she had a flat. Or two."

"But you guys carried spare tubes, right? Tools?"

"Of course. But it's not like the Tour de France or anything. No team car drives up with a spare bike. We had to change them ourselves, and it takes time—especially if it's the rear tire with the bike chain and the gears."

Ryan rubbed both hands across his face, wishing he could erase the images cluttering his mind. Jenna out riding her Schwinn bicycle. Her surprise at the flat tire. She'd glance back and sigh as she glided over to the side of the road, unclipping one shoe out of the pedals. Coming to a stop, assessing the situation, pulling out her repair kit.

All that time alone on the side of a road that *should* have been safe. But somebody had pulled over, and instead of helping, they'd attacked and killed her.

"Why did she go riding alone?" The question ripped out of his heart almost unconsciously. "You guys always went together. Why didn't she ask you, Laney?"

FOURTEEN

Laney thought she might be sick. Her melting ice cream with its chunks of Butterfinger candy mocked her for eating so much as the question she'd been dreading echoed through her mind.

Hadn't she always known things would come to this place? That God wouldn't let her keep her secrets buried forever?

The hurt etched across Ryan's face was nearly enough to break her heart. Tears sprang into her eyes and she shook her head, wishing she could make the terrible truth of that day vanish.

But nothing would drive it away, and if she didn't tell him, the truth would burn inside her like an inferno ready to swallow her whole. She opened her mouth, willing the words to come out. "She did ask me."

"And? You couldn't go? I don't get it."

Her esophagus burned. "I told her to go without me."

"But why, Laney?" He held both hands out, open, as if he could argue his sister back to life. As if wresting the truth out of her could undo the past.

"Ryan…" Why was it so hard to say? If only God

would whisk her away right now to anywhere but here. "I was throwing up."

He frowned. "Okay… So she could wait a day or two for you to feel better. Didn't you guys ride indoors on those spinning things sometimes? I thought Jenna borrowed them from a friend in Bloomington."

"Rollers?" Frustration knotted up her insides. Shouldn't he understand by now? It wasn't like she had gotten into that mess by herself. "Morning sickness, Ryan. I had morning sickness. And I couldn't tell your sister because then she'd tell your parents, and you and I would've ended up as teenage parents raising a kid in a ramshackle trailer. Just like my mother." Tears pricked her eyes as the words flowed out, like poison being released by her body. "I panicked. I told her to go without me, even though she offered to wait. Even though the truth would've come out eventually."

She dropped her head onto her crossed arms so she wouldn't have to see whatever horrified expression had crossed his face. "It's my fault she went alone. It's my fault she's dead."

It was out. Emotion drained from her, like a bucket of water dumped onto dry ground, until she felt empty and wasted inside. Sure, God had forgiven her—she knew *that*—but the Mitchells never would. Probably those girls at the next table had heard her confession, too, and soon the whole town would know.

The wooden picnic table creaked, and its balance shifted as Ryan stood. Maybe he was so upset he'd leave her here with her misery. She pressed her forehead onto the chipping red paint and rough woodgrain of the table.

His hand touched the back of her head, fingers tugging through her hair in a gentle caress. He sat heavily on the bench next to her. "Laney, look at me."

"No." Maybe it was childish, but she'd forsaken any pretense of maturity a few minutes ago when she'd confessed.

"Laney." The word came out strangled, like he couldn't decide what to feel. Anger? Agony? Loathing? But the way his hand cupped the back of her head was heart-wrenchingly gentle. "Look at me. Please."

It wasn't the words as much as the way he'd said them, like he was desperate to reach her. She'd barely been able to walk away from him ten years ago. How could she turn him down now? When she finally forced her gaze to meet his, the storm of emotion in his eyes nearly swept her away. Pain, yes. Grief. But not only for himself. Something else eclipsed the rest—care for *her*.

Maybe even…love?

"You were pregnant?" he whispered. "What happened?"

She swiped at the tears tracking down her cheeks. How ridiculous, crying at Dairy Queen with her ex-boyfriend. Exactly the horrible nightmare she'd wanted to avoid, and yet…

And yet telling him had eased the burden she'd carried for ten long years. Maybe even *this* ugly mess could be redeemed by God's grace.

"Miscarriage. It happened the next week, after Jenna vanished. I wasn't far along, maybe six weeks."

Those two weeks had been some of the worst in her life. First the positive pregnancy test, then Jenna vanishing and then the terrible cramping that told her something was desperately wrong. She'd had to invent a whole story about food poisoning to explain to her mother why she'd visited the local urgent care center. There was nothing they could do anyway, beyond sending her home with acetaminophen.

"Why didn't you tell me?" Ryan's tone wasn't reproachful, more comforting than anything. "You know I would've done anything for you."

"We were eighteen, Ryan." She tilted her head to one side, still reliving the dread of that summer. The loss, the guilt, the sense of relief so intense it made her feel ashamed. "I was terrified. And I couldn't see beyond my mother, my own childhood. I couldn't let that happen. So after I lost the baby—"

He raised his eyebrows. "That's why you left."

She nodded. "I stuck around long enough to wait for word on Jenna. And when they gave up the search, I got out of here as fast as I could."

"To make a life for yourself."

"Yes." She stared down at her hands. "I'm sorry, Ryan. I'm so sorry about Jenna and that I didn't have the courage to tell you the truth. I'm sorry for leaving the way I did."

"You did what you thought was best. I get that. And I wondered for so long if it was my fault." He placed his hand against her cheek, and she met his gaze as he wiped away a stray tear with his thumb. The heat of his skin and the strength of his hand felt comforting and reassuring. "I guess it was, in a way. Will you forgive me too?"

"I already have. But what about Jenna? About me letting her go alone?"

"Laney, no one can snatch us out of the Lord's hands before our time. Even though I don't understand why He allowed that to happen to my family, I trust Him. If for nothing else, He used my grief to bring me to salvation."

She quirked her lips into a crooked smile. "Me, too, actually. I never would've turned to faith if all of this hadn't happened. Jenna must be so relieved up there in heaven, knowing we finally came around."

"Come here," he said, pulling her close. His strong arms formed a cocoon against the world, and for a brief moment, she was eighteen again, pregnant and scared but not alone. Never alone. Because God had been with her even then, and He'd provided for her in more ways than she could've imagined.

Ryan and his family had been one of those means of provision. He'd meant the world to her then, and she knew beyond a doubt he could easily take that place in her life again if she was willing to let him. If he wanted the same thing.

When his arms relaxed and she pulled back, she found she couldn't tear her eyes away from his. Dairy Queen and the rest of Sandy Bluff vanished as Ryan leaned closer. Their lips touched—the slightest brush of a kiss, a whisper of hope for the future.

But then he pulled back, shaking his head. "I'm sorry, Laney. I wasn't thinking. We agreed nothing would happen, and I respect you and your decision. I *have* matured since I was eighteen."

"Of course." Her cheeks grew hot, but it wasn't embarrassment over his apology—it was from the way that kiss had made her heart thrum beneath her rib cage. "Don't worry about it, Ryan. Thanks for forgiving me."

He looked very much like he wanted to touch her again—a kiss to the forehead or fingers against her cheek—but he merely nodded and stood. "I'm glad we could clear the air. Shall we get going?"

As she walked with him back to the car, Laney couldn't

help wondering if she was the only one beginning to re-gret their decision to avoid a romantic relationship.

Ryan desperately longed to get home and find some space to think, to wrap his mind around everything Laney had just told him. How little he'd understood all those years ago when she left. He'd nearly been a *father*.

Technically, he supposed, he *was* a father, only his little one hadn't made it. The thought left an unexpected crater in his already-injured heart.

And here was Laney, back again, getting into the car next to him, and he would have to let her walk out of his life. After everything, he owed her that much, didn't he? The freedom to choose her own path, without him trying to persuade her to stay.

No matter how much it hurt.

Silence settled over them as he pulled the car out of the parking lot to head back to his parents' house. What was there to say after that conversation? Or that kiss?

He smacked a palm against the steering wheel, ig-noring the sideways glance Laney gave him. *Stupid*—that's what that kiss had been. She'd said she forgave him, but their relationship was so damaged, so fragile, he shouldn't be taking any steps that might break the tiny connection they'd forged.

Thinking about Laney would have to wait until he was alone. For now, it was better to focus on the case. "I'll talk to my father tonight about searching the bog for the other set of remains, using that map."

She glanced up from her hands, where she'd been pick-ing her fingernails. No doubt sharing his same sense of uncertainty about their relationship. "The remains from the Wilson case should make it to my lab by tomorrow.

They'll do a comparison with Jenna's remains and let us know if my soft analysis is correct."

Ryan turned off the main road where Dairy Queen stood among Sandy Bluff's other meager national-chain offerings and headed onto one of the county highways that looped around town toward his parents' neighborhood. Evening was approaching quickly, and the thick clouds that had been building since morning had become a dense gray mass blanketing the sky. Lightning flickered in the west, illuminating entire sections of the storm clouds.

"Did you see that?" he asked after a particularly huge bolt tracked through the clouds. The thunder reached them a few seconds later.

"Yeah." Laney leaned forward in her seat, watching the sky through the front windshield. "Looks like it's going to pour."

The first few drops followed almost immediately, then the downpour. A typical Midwest cats-and-dogs-type rain shower but hopefully without the tornado sirens.

The lights were off inside his parents' house—odd, considering his mother would normally be preparing dinner by now—and the storm had muted the usual summer-evening brightness. Or if she'd decided to order takeout, she'd at least be reading in the living room. It was a little early yet for his father to be home.

After shutting off the engine, he led the way through the garage and side door. "Mom?"

No answer. Her car was still in the garage, but maybe she'd gone out for a walk, hoping to avoid the storm.

"Where is she?" Laney asked.

He flipped on the lights in the back hallway at the

same moment his foot pressed down on something. His brain recognized it as a button, almost like a Christmas-tree light switch, and simultaneously, his ears registered the click.

Another bomb.

FIFTEEN

"Laney, get out!" he yelled. He shoved her toward the still-open door into the garage as the bomb went off. The force of the explosion flung them out onto the hard concrete. Bits of drywall and wood shrapnel flew in all directions, pelting against his still-tender back like hail. Outside, thunder crackled and then exploded like a second bomb.

Laney stirred beside him, and he sat back on his knees, stretching shaking fingers to touch her shoulder and her hair.

"Are you okay?" he asked, shouting over the ringing in his ears. Praise God that the door to the garage had still been open. Otherwise...

She sat up, dabbing her fingers against her forehead, then pressing her hands to her ears. "Yeah, I think so." Her lips moved, but the sound seemed like it was coming from a mile away.

He ran his fingers lightly up her arms, feeling for any injuries or breaks. Satisfied she was still whole, he pulled her against his chest. She didn't resist.

She slipped her arms around his back, and he leaned his cheek on her soft, short hair, filling his senses with the light fragrance of peaches from her shampoo. They stayed that way for a long moment, until the ringing had started to clear in his ears and Laney pulled away.

His knees were wobbly as he forced himself to rise. "I've got to check on Mom."

Laney pressed her hand to her mouth. "Of course."

Pieces of the door frame dangled from loose nails, and an entire section of drywall had been blasted out to reveal the wooden beams beneath.

Thankfully, the kitchen lights came on when he flipped the switch, bathing the kitchen in light. Sometime in the last few minutes, the downpour had diminished from a continual pounding to a gentle rain, and the thunder boomed farther to the east.

"Do you hear that?" Laney asked, her dark eyes alert.

Intermittent thumps were coming from the hallway on the far side of the living room, the one that led to the bedrooms. His gaze collided with hers for a second, then they both dashed across the carpet, dodging the sofa table and recliners. Laney turned on the hall light. The only door that was shut was the one for the guest bath.

"Mom?" Ryan called, twisting the knob. Locked.

More thumps came in reply, shaking the wall. She had to be on the other side.

"Get back, I'm going to break down the door!"

"Wait, Ryan," Laney interrupted. She stretched on tiptoe, just barely reaching the top of the frame to come away with a small, straight brass key in her hand. "Here."

Right. No need to breach the door after all. He pushed the key into the knob and popped the lock open.

"Mom?" He dropped to his knees on the floor beside her. She lay on her side, hands tied behind her back, feet bound at the ankles. A rag had been stuffed into her mouth and secured at the back of her head.

Laney was next to her in a heartbeat, lifting Mary's head onto her lap and working at the tight knot with her fingers. Together they removed the bindings and helped his mother out to a recliner in the living room, where she sat fanning herself with a trembling hand.

"My word." Mary leaned forward, resting her head on her knees. Ryan rubbed her back gently, offering a silent prayer of gratitude that she hadn't been injured. "What happened? That wasn't thunder."

"It was a bomb." He held up his hands as her eyes went wide. "We're okay, though, and the house will be fine after some minor repairs."

"I'll make you some tea," Laney offered. By the time she returned with the steaming mug, Mary had managed to sit back up, though she still shook like a kettle at full boil.

"I'm so glad you two are all right," she murmured. Laney crouched beside her, offering the tea, and Mary took a tentative sip.

"I'm going to call Dad," Ryan said, pulling out his cell phone. His father's anger reverberated back from the other end of the line. A second attack on their home, and this one had put more than Laney's life in danger. When he hung up, he turned back to his mother. "Dad says he's on his way. What happened?"

"I was working on supper, and then the doorbell rang—"

"Mom!" he interrupted. "You didn't open up, did you?" Hadn't they gone over this before? How she had to be more cautious than ordinary folks on account of her husband being police chief?

"I'm sorry. I didn't think." At least some of the color

was returning to her round cheeks. "I assumed it was a neighbor. The storm made it dark and hard to see, and whoever it was wasn't large."

"Was it a man or a woman?"

"I couldn't tell, but based on size, I'd guess a woman," Mary said. Laney glanced at him, mouthing the words *Kathleen Kincaide*. His mother continued, "She had a dark hood pulled up—I figured it was because of the rain. I only opened the door a crack, but she shoved inside. She had a gun."

Anger twisted inside his chest. First Laney's mother, then Laney herself and now his mom? They *had* to catch whoever was behind these attacks. "Did she hurt you?"

"No. But I cooperated. I didn't realize she'd leave a bomb."

Laney squeezed Mary's hand. "You did the right thing. You didn't get hurt, and neither did we."

"Did the suspect say what she wanted?" Ryan asked.

Mary shook her head. "Only that I wouldn't get hurt if I did what she said."

By the time his father arrived home, Mary had more or less made a full recovery. Mom had always been sturdy like that—reminded him of Laney, actually. Both women were tough as nails, each in her own way. While they sat together drinking tea, Ryan pulled his father aside.

"Dad, maybe I should get Laney out of here. I hate that Mom's been put in danger."

Jim let out a long breath but shook his head. "Laney's family to us, Ryan. She's safer here than anywhere else you could take her, short of sending her home. I'll assign a plainclothes officer as an extra patrol."

Laney must've seen them whispering together, because she left Mary and came to join them on the far end of the kitchen. "Did you tell him about the map?"

Jim raised an eyebrow, and Ryan fished the map out of his pocket. His father cast a quick glance at him. "Very odd, indeed. Why give you this, but then plant a bomb in our house?"

"Based on what happened at the airport, we're dealing with two people," Ryan said. "A man and possibly a woman. We're still waiting on confirmation from the forensics, but we think we'll be able to prove Ronald Wilson was framed and that the real killer is still at large." He filled in his father on the getaway truck and the other evidence they'd found. "So the question is, what do we do now?"

Jim cracked his knuckles, staring at the floor for a moment. "Here's what I think. Fake Laney's departure, and then you two lie low for a couple of days while we wait on lab results. In the meantime, I'll get a team to poke around the bog and see what they can find. There's no reason to throw yourselves in harm's way."

The plan was solid. Ryan nodded. "Sounds good."

The next few days felt *heavy* to Laney, for lack of any better way to describe them. Like thick gray clouds burdened with rain, each passing moment seemed to foretell impending danger.

She and Ryan made a public show of Laney saying goodbye at the police station, packing up her meager belongings in a new tote bag from the store and driving to the airport. Actually, they went only about halfway before he decided they weren't being followed and it was safe to circle back. They'd chosen a morning when Lawrence Brown wasn't on shift, just to make sure he couldn't track Laney inside the airport.

She spent the time hidden away in the Mitchells' home, behind closed curtains, always with either Jim or Ryan or another officer assigned to keep guard. It felt like house arrest, and by the time the third day arrived, she was seriously contemplating breaking parole before she went crazy.

By late afternoon, it was Ryan's turn to take over the watch. Laney slumped on the basement sofa, flipping through channels on the television but not really paying attention to anything that came on. Between repairs to the house and working the case, he hadn't been around much over the preceding days—popping in to check on her and give updates but not staying long enough to renew anything close to the conversation they'd shared over ice cream.

She couldn't avoid the thought that maybe he didn't *want* to be around her. That regardless of his assurances to the contrary, maybe he couldn't forgive her. The possibility niggled deep into her heart, like a thorn stuck in a lion's paw, creating an ache with each step. But wasn't that what she wanted? To close the door on this chapter of her life?

But the more she was around Ryan, the more she doubted that was possible. Long-forgotten feelings had been dusted off and spruced up and now demanded her attention. She'd been head over heels in love once, and those feelings hadn't gone away—they'd only matured into a deeper, more powerful connection that time and geography hadn't erased.

As he thumped down the basement stairs, she roused herself from her slump on the couch.

"Hey," she called over her shoulder, twisting toward the steps.

He wore his uniform, having just come from work. Judging from the dark circles beneath his eyes, he felt as weary as she did. "Hey." When he plopped down beside her, placing both hands on top of his head, the cushion tilted so that she leaned closer.

"Did you see the report from my lab?" she asked. One of her colleagues had emailed the file to her earlier in the day, copying it to Ryan.

He nodded. "Same killer, different weapons—proving Wilson was framed. How can you guys tell stuff like that?"

"Bones never lie. It's amazing what you can see at a microscopic level. The mark a weapon makes is determined by its surface and weight, the angle and force of impact, and the type of motion, among other things." She smiled. "It's beautifully logical, unlike most of life."

"Wilson's lawyer called me back."

"And?"

"Wilson blamed Lawrence Brown, same as Kincaide. Claimed they spent years playing poker together every weekend with a crew of some other locals. I got the names."

"Well, that's good news." Why did Ryan still sound dejected? "It confirms our suspicions."

"But I talked to the warden about Wilson's contacts, and he had only one call from Kathleen Kincaide right after he was incarcerated, then nothing. No Lawrence Brown at all. As convenient as it is to point the finger at them, Laney, we don't even have enough evidence for an arrest warrant, much less to win a court case."

"Could they have used fake names to check on him?"

"Maybe, but that's not enough to go on." He let out a sigh, giving Laney the gnawing suspicion he had more bad news to share. After a long moment, he went on, "The chief gave the go ahead to search the bog for the other set of remains."

She jerked upright, excitement driving out the somber disappointment of a moment before. "Then why do you look so gloomy? Let's get out there and collect them."

He'd been staring at the wall unit opposite them, with its large television bracketed by bookcases, but at her words, his brown gaze darted to her face. Worry crinkled around his eyes. "No, Laney. You can't. We'll do it ourselves. Or bring in somebody else."

"Why—"

Now he sat upright, taking both her hands into his, triggering a cascade of flutters through her stomach. "Because the *killer* gave us that information. He's after *you*, Laney. Why else would he do it?"

She squeezed his hands, then pulled her own from his grasp. "That's what I thought, too, but then why bother planting a bomb here in your house?"

He ran his hands over his forehead and through his dark hair. "It doesn't make sense to me, either, but I can't think of any other reason he'd give us those remains. Maybe he's trying to scare you into doing something reckless. Regardless, you're in danger."

"Hey," she said, touching his cheek lightly. "My life is in the Lord's hands. Same as yours. I won't take any unnecessary risks."

He clenched his fist and turned away. "It gets worse."

Something about his tone made her stomach drop. "What?"

"We've got a lead on Madison Smith."

"Your missing college student?"

Ryan held out a large manila envelope she hadn't noticed before. "This arrived at the station today in the mail, addressed to me." His jaw muscles tightened.

She opened the envelope and pulled out a single large photograph. A twentysomething blond-haired girl sat bound to a chair, duct tape across her mouth, her eyes red and puffy from tears, cheeks stained with dried blood. Behind her was a plank wall, almost like an old barn, with vertical boards covered in fading yellow paint. And at her feet, resting against her legs, stood a white sign with the same scrawled handwriting she'd seen far too often.

Your choice: you or her.

Tomorrow at dawn. Come alone.

The sinking feeling in her stomach opened into a pit. She had no doubt whom this message was for, and it wasn't Ryan.

"Oh, Ryan…" she murmured, unable to stop staring at the girl's face. The way her hair hung in clumps around her red, tear-streaked cheeks. The bruises on her exposed arms.

He pressed his hand to his forehead again, leaning one elbow on his knee. "It's Madison Smith. Verified by facial recognition software, but we'll confirm with her mother." How awful, to have to share this photograph with the girl's family. "Look at the time stamp on the photograph."

"Two days ago?" Laney's heart hurt. "That was after I supposedly left."

"Yeah. Guess our ruse didn't work." His hair stood up on end from the way he kept running his hands through it. She'd rarely seen him this upset.

What she had to say next wasn't going to make things better.

Fear rattled her insides, but the certainty that she was doing the right thing made her declaration easier. "You know I can't let her die."

"Of course we won't let her die. We'll figure out where he has her."

"After we figure out who he is?" Laney asked gently. Ryan wasn't quite getting her point. "We don't have that kind of time."

He pulled his hands away from his head to stare at her, dark brows pulling together. "What are you trying to say?"

"You're going to use me as bait."

SIXTEEN

Ryan's chest constricted like it was caught in a vise. "No, Laney, you are staying as far away from that killer as humanly possible."

"Hear me out." She had that hard look in her eye that spelled *stubborn*. "You have an amazing team of police officers behind you. You guys can rig me up with one of those cool tracking gadgets like they use in the spy movies, and then once you've tracked us to the girl's location, you can swoop in and get me out."

"Laney, this isn't a TV cop show. Sure, we've got some tools at our disposal, but there's no guarantee things would go according to plan. You could *die*." Anguish tore at his insides. After everything they'd already gone through, how could God let it come to this?

"That's a risk I'm willing to take, both for Madison Smith and for your sister."

"Jenna's already gone. I can't lose you too."

"But her death demands justice." She stood, apparently unable to sit still any longer, and paced back and forth in front of the television. Meaningless commercials advertised summer patio sets on clearance, a painful contrast to the real world and the lives at stake. "Maybe this is how God will accomplish it, through you and me. Who better to stand up for her?"

He rose from the couch, too, positioning himself directly in front of her. If only there was some way to get through to her. "I can't let you do this. The last ten years without you nearly crushed me. And I know we agreed not to pursue a relationship, and you don't owe me anything in the future. But I don't think I could stand living, knowing I'd been the cause of your death."

She offered a small, crooked grin. "Who says I'm going to die? You've always been there for me. You won't let me down now. The Lord watches over His righteous ones. Even if the worst happens, I'll be safe with Him in heaven. Like Jenna is."

Every cell in his body rebelled against this idea. "We haven't exhausted our leads yet. I'll send the K-9 team to Kathleen Kincaide's. We're still waiting on the DNA results from the inside of the truck. Maybe it will give us the evidence we need."

"We don't have that kind of time, Ryan. Not unless you want another body on your hands."

As much as he hated the thought of putting her life in danger, she had a point. "We don't know where to find him. Where would you go?"

"He told me where. The map marking the remains, remember? Why else would he have given it to me?"

His jaw tightened until a muscle twitched. "You want me to leave you alone in the bog? Waiting for a serial killer to come take you?"

"Yes." A flicker of fear darted across her face, but she squared her shoulders with typical Laney determination. It was just like her, offering to put her own life on the line to save someone else. For once, he wished she wasn't quite so admirable.

"We need to discuss this idea with my father. I won't agree without his input."

She held a hand toward the staircase. "Then let's go."

He could barely keep it together as he escorted Laney into the police station early the next morning. While he agreed on a rational level that the plan was sound, his heart revolted against what was coming. But Chief Mitchell had given his approval, and from the grim set to Laney's jaw, she was determined to see it through. Still, he couldn't help but wonder if his father's determination to get justice for Jenna wasn't clouding his judgment about Laney.

So here he was, against his own personal wishes, taking her to the equipment room to get hooked up with a tracker, an earpiece and a tiny mic. There was nothing for it now but to put on a brave face for Laney's sake.

And pray.

"Here's the tracker." He handed her a flat silver square resembling a nicotine patch. "It's got an adhesive back. Peel off this backing and stick it somewhere no one will notice." Turning his back, he waited.

"Done." Her face was calm, but dark circles lined the undersides of her eyes. Apparently he wasn't the only one who hadn't been able to sleep last night.

"Now tuck this into your ear."

She accepted the tiny earpiece, holding it up between two fingertips. "It looks like a wireless earbud."

"Pretty much. We want to upgrade all our tech to wireless, but it's expensive." He winked—half-heartedly, but a wink all the same. "So don't lose it."

Her lips tried to tilt into a smile, but it didn't reach her eyes. "I won't."

The mic was still hardwired to a battery case she'd have to wear at her waist. Ryan helped her attach it to her belt, then conceal it beneath her shirt. He stood back to examine her, frowning at the bulky box showing through her thin sweatshirt.

"Here." He slipped off his police-issue black jacket. "You can wear this. It's cool enough this morning to be believable."

"Thanks, Ryan." She slid it on, then held up both arms to show how her hands had vanished inside the sleeves. His heart twinged. "It's a little big."

"Just a bit." He helped her roll up the sleeves before glancing at his watch.

"Is it time?"

He nodded. "Do you want to take a collection kit? To give you something to do while you're out there?"

She shrugged. "Might as well."

He let his gaze roam over her face—those bright, daring eyes, her pert nose, her pretty cheekbones. Would they have a moment like this again?

God, protect her. Please. They'd prayed together last night after talking to his father and then again on the way here. But extra prayers never hurt.

She blushed and glanced away. "Stop looking at me like that. You'll see me again. I'm not that easy to shake."

Despite everything, he grinned. "No, you're not."

He pulled her into a fierce embrace for a long moment, then released her to look into her face again. "Laney, I need you to know something." His chest hitched, but he swallowed back down the fear and uncertainty. "I've never stopped loving you. You're a part of me, and you always will be, no matter what happens."

Maybe it was foolish to tell her now, and so bluntly, but he didn't want a lifetime of regret for having held back. No matter how she felt about him in return.

Her expression softened until she looked almost wistful, and then she sighed as she stared at his shirt. His chest deflated.

"Ryan, I—"

"You two ready?" His father appeared in the doorway.

Her mouth hung open a fraction of a second before she clamped it shut and turned to Jim. "As ready as I'm going to be."

Ryan waved weakly at her. "She's got the tracker and the mic. We just need to test it."

"Great. Let's do it." The chief moved aside to let Laney and Ryan pass. "Ryan, you and Henderson will follow and stay parked out of sight. We've got three other teams already in position. Laney, you can borrow my car and leave it parked on the dirt road."

Together they walked out to the parking lot. Laney loaded her case of collection tools into the trunk and accepted the keys Jim held out.

"God go with you, Laney," he said.

She smiled grimly. "And you all. Thanks, Jim."

He squeezed both of them on the shoulders. "Well, I'll leave you two to get started. Ryan, keep me updated."

"Yes, sir." He waited in silence beside Laney for a long moment as his father walked back inside. Part of him wanted to ask what she'd been about to say a moment ago in the equipment room, but somehow the timing felt wrong. So instead, he hugged her again, this time pressing a kiss to her forehead when they pulled apart.

"Ready?" he asked one more time, searching her face for the answer.

She nodded, her jaw set. The same determination he'd seen in those eyes so many times sparked to life again.

"Then let's test your mic and get you on your way."

With a final squeeze of her hand, Ryan stood back and waited as she climbed behind the wheel of the car. Then he turned for the surveillance van, praying desperately that this wasn't the last time he'd see the only girl who'd ever held his heart.

The sun was creeping toward the horizon—Laney could see a faint orange hue breaking the twilight above the trees ahead as she headed east toward the bog. Somewhere behind, Ryan sat in a police van keeping a watchful eye on the situation. While that certainty brought a measure of comfort, nothing could stop the fear paralyzing her insides.

She lifted her chin a fraction higher. For the sake of the poor girl who'd been taken and to catch a killer, she could do this.

Even if her heart was doing flip-flops inside her chest.

Of course, part of that was Ryan's fault. His words rang through her mind as she left behind the last traces of Sandy Bluff's commercial zones and turned onto the highway that would lead her to the bog.

You're a part of me, and you always will be.

How foolish she'd been to think she could come back here, see him again and *not* have her life thrown upside down. Her heart had wanted so desperately to say the same things back to him at that moment. Their lives had become intertwined as children, and nothing short of death could ever separate them. She gripped the steering wheel as dread constricted her muscles.

If she got out of this predicament alive, maybe then she could tell him.

Or perhaps it was for the best that Jim had interrupted. Because was she ready to give up her new life and come back to Sandy Bluff, after everything she'd done to escape?

No. Coming back here would always feel like a metaphorical return to her mother's trailer. No matter how much she loved Ryan.

She ignored the way her heart twisted in protest and instead focused on each turn of the highway as she left Sandy Bluff behind. The road was as familiar again as if she still lived here. There was the big white farmhouse with the sagging front porch. Her throat closed, and she forced in a deep breath. Almost there.

Around the bend, the road dipped and a valley draped in thick fog opened before her. The bog was down there, buried beneath that fog like a body lost to memory beneath the dirt. A shiver tickled her spine. Woods masked the rising sun to the east, leaving only a vague pinkish-orange blush over the horizon.

The road vanished into white mist. Laney slowed the car, double checking the headlights were on. The last thing she needed was to die in a head-on collision before she even reached the bog.

Besides, the dirt road would be easy to miss in these conditions.

She flipped on her turn signal when she saw the narrow opening to the right, creating an eerie blinking orange that glowed too close, like the fog had become a living thing hemming in her car.

The car jostled as the tires rolled onto the bumpy road. It had been, what, six days since she'd come out here with Ryan? What she wouldn't give to have him at her side right now.

"I'm pulling onto the dirt road," she said softly into the mic. "Can you hear me?"

"Yeah, Laney, I've got you." Ryan's familiar voice came through the earpiece, a tiny measure of comfort to ease the trembling in her hands. He'd always been there for her, until she pushed him away. Even after what she'd done, leaving him like that, he'd never withheld his love from her.

The thought warmed her heart as she pulled the car to a stop and killed the engine.

"Laney, we're going silent on this end so he doesn't notice your earpiece." He paused, and for a moment, unspoken words seemed to hover in her ear, but then the radio clicked off.

"Okay," she answered.

She clutched Ryan's jacket around her as she stepped out of the car. Fog pressed close in eddying waves, so that one moment she could see fifteen feet into the bog, and the next, she could barely see the car door as she closed it. The latching sound seemed to die instantly. Running one hand along the cool metal, she walked around the vehicle to the passenger side and pulled out the collection kit. Her boots crunched against the gravel until she reached the mucky edge of the bog.

Hip waders wouldn't work today. Not when she was acting as bait for a serial killer. They'd impede her movement and make her claustrophobic. Instead, she'd keep to the thick clumps of moss as she worked her way out into the bog.

She tipped her head down toward the mic. "Heading out into the field." It'd be her last intentional communication with Ryan.

Maybe forever.

There was so much more she could say, more she *wanted* to say, but not now. Not in front of the other officers and not with what she still had to do.

Her heart rate increased with each slurping, muddy step into the soggy field. The air smelled of rotting vegetation and wet earth and mist. As the sun rose above the tree line on the far side, shafts of light penetrated the fog, revealing dark, skinny arms of bushes and short trees like so many skeletons.

Was he watching her already? Lurking somewhere in this thick pea soup, waiting to leap out of nowhere? Would he crush in part of her skull, the way he had Jenna's?

A tremor ran through her body, and she took a long, steadying breath. Unhelpful thoughts. Whatever happened, she needed to be here, both so they could catch the killer and to help that poor, terrified girl who was still alive.

Resolve gave her shaking spine a bit of needed strength. Using the intermittent lighter patches of fog, when she could make out the tall trees on the far side of the field, she traipsed out until she could see the yellow police tape still around the site where they'd excavated Jenna's remains. She dug the killer's map out of her pocket and studied it for a moment, always listening for any indication of someone else out in this forlorn place. Maybe it was too early. Maybe he wouldn't expect her to be out here yet.

According to the map, she needed to head southeast by about fifteen paces to reach the second set of remains.

Might as well see if she could find anything. It wasn't like she had anything better to do.

She checked herself before she accidentally told Ryan what she was doing. He'd know from the tracker stuck to her stomach like a giant Band-Aid. In the distance, a car drove past on the road, the whir of its engine drifting ominously through the fog.

Fifteen paces through the muck brought her past the halfway point of the field and closer to the far tree line. What lay over there in those woods? When they were teens, the land had belonged to an adjoining farm, but would it now, after so many years? It still gave off the same abandoned, desolate air. The perfect place for killers to hide.

Frowning, she dropped the collection kit on the ground near a cluster of bushes and scanned the field again, or what little of it she could see—nothing more than maybe ten feet in each direction. Had she even gone the right direction from the other set of remains? Still, there was nothing else to do but poke around in the ground, hunting for any sign of evidence.

Seconds slipped into minutes as she examined the terrain at her feet. Depending on how long the remains had been here, and how many times the field had frozen over and thawed, they could either have worked their way deeper or closer to the surface. There—that spot where the vegetation grew unevenly near the base of one of the scraggly bushes looked promising. She'd seen a similar site in a swampy location near the Chesapeake Bay, where remains had been buried in silt along a river and the plants had grown in an irregular pattern.

Laney carried her collection kit closer and crouched near the bush. Pulling out a trowel, she dug carefully near some milkweed roots, her breath catching as she scraped against something hard about an inch beneath the surface. Gently she pressed cold fingertips into the mud, feeling for the object. Long and thin and with the distinctive texture of only one material.

Bone.

A soft rustling nearby made her sit up abruptly. She'd become so absorbed in searching she'd nearly forgotten why she was out in a bog all alone. And she certainly hadn't been listening as intently as she had earlier.

Laney's heart hammered as she glanced automatically over her shoulder, as if the only way a serial killer approached a victim was from behind.

But he didn't come from behind.

He stepped around the bush where she'd been digging, a smile on his face that twisted her stomach.

Lawrence Brown.

"I knew you'd find me." He pointed at the ground where the tip of a bone now protruded from the mud, and his smile widened. "And her. I'm so glad to see you again, Laney Hamilton."

SEVENTEEN

"Brown." Ryan pointed at the speaker in the back of the department's surveillance van. His stomach churned. "It's Lawrence Brown. I *knew* it."

He'd known from the moment he'd gotten that man into the interrogation room, yet he'd had to release him. And now Laney was out there alone with him.

He tapped the barrier separating the surveillance equipment from the driver, then rotated his finger even though Henderson couldn't see. But he'd hear over the intercom. "Get us moving." Punching a couple of buttons, he connected with his father. "Chief, based on voice recognition, it's Lawrence Brown. Permission to move in?"

"Negative, Sergeant Mitchell," Jim's voice crackled over the speaker. "We need to secure the other victim. Follow, but do not engage."

"Copy," Ryan replied. Much as he wanted to swoop in and rescue Laney, his father was right. They were playing the long game.

And there was still the matter of Brown's accomplice, the woman. It had to be Kathleen Kincaide. She could've convinced her brother to plant the bomb in Laney's suitcase and then hid the components in her ex-husband's garage herself. After stealing his truck.

But where was she now? And how would they prove her involvement?

He reached for the radio again. "Update Officer McIntosh on Lawrence Brown. She's en route to search Kathleen Kincaide's house and might need backup."

But if her intent had been to scare Laney away, did she know about Lawrence's scheme to claim her as his next victim? Were they working at cross purposes?

Laney's ragged breath coming through the mic pulled his thoughts back to the bog where she stood unarmed with the man who'd killed his sister. "But the dog didn't find—"

Her voice vanished into a crackle of static. Ryan glanced sharply at their technician, Gabby Walters, as she flipped a couple of switches.

A second later, Laney's line went dead.

He clenched his jaw. "What happened?"

"We lost her." Gabby shook her head. "My guess is either the mic fell out or he found it."

It had always been a possibility, but a knot tightened in Ryan's chest anyway. He watched the flashing red dot representing Laney's tracker on the computer screen. What if Brown didn't take her to the other victim? What if he killed her right there?

The red blip started to move. He pictured the bog in his mind, imagining Brown's hand clamped around Laney's slender arm, dragging her through the muck. Each step sent a shiver of fear rippling through his back.

Their van wasn't far from the field, but each passing second felt agonizingly long as he watched the blip move toward the tree line on the eastern border of the bog.

"They stopped again," the tech said as the red marker paused on the screen. "Why?"

Ryan sucked at his lower lip. No way would Brown kill her right there in the field, not with the way the fog was lifting. Too exposed. "I don't know. Unless…"

He watched the red light flash on and off, perfectly rhythmic, perfectly still. The knot in his stomach tightened as his sense of certainty grew. "Unless he found the tracker too."

Gabby turned questioning eyes on Ryan.

He swallowed. "We've got people in position to watch for a vehicle while Henderson and I track her on foot. We'll call in the dogs if we have to."

The van slowed, and Ryan's seat rattled as they pulled off onto an unpaved road. Henderson's voice came through the speaker. "Fog's thinned too much to park next to the field, so I pulled off across the road. Walters can monitor us from here."

Ryan unbuckled and stood, double-checking his gear as Henderson pulled the back door open. He popped an earpiece into his ear and handed a second to Henderson. A moment later, they stepped out into the muggy morning air.

Henderson had parked the truck on a dirt lane deep in the trees. Ryan jogged the short distance back to the county highway, his partner following close behind. The fog had thinned enough to reveal a ribbon of black asphalt stretching toward the hills to the east, but clumps of white mist still lingered over Waltman's Bog a quarter mile away. At least it would help hide their approach.

The air felt unnaturally still as they crossed the road and hastened along the shallow ditch at the side.

When they reached the dirt road running along the western edge of the bog, Gabby's hushed voice came through Ryan's earpiece. "No signs of any vehicle leaving the area."

Good. That meant Brown and Laney were still close. He tapped his mic three times to indicate he'd heard the message, then nodded at Henderson. *Let's go.*

He led the way into the bog, heading straight for where the map indicated they'd find the other remains. And apparently she had. Laney's collection kit sat on a mound of moss. She'd exposed the top of a bone in the ground. He shook his head. Just like Laney—trying to get some work done while she waited for a serial killer.

Something small and black caught his eye. Laney's mic, caught in the fringe of a bush. Her earpiece dangled from another branch nearby. A lump formed in his throat, but he swallowed it back down as he searched the ground for footprints. She'd had the tracker on for another hundred feet at least, and he knew the direction they'd taken. But once they reached her tracker, they'd be on their own.

Henderson tapped Ryan's elbow and pointed to the ground a few feet away. In the mud, the heel of a boot was clearly visible—Laney's, judging by the size. Her direction of travel matched what they'd seen from the tracker. Ryan took the lead, stepping gingerly around Laney's print and scanning the ground as he followed her trail. Each step in the mucky field felt too loud, but maybe it didn't matter.

Brown had found the tracker. He would know the police were looking, that it was only a matter of time.

Would he hurry to kill Laney?

Ryan's stomach twisted, and he picked up his pace, following the diagonal route across the field until they'd reached the approximate place where the tracker had stopped. The tech's voice came softly through his earpiece. "You're at the tracker."

He surveyed the ground at his feet, but it was nowhere to be seen. Not surprising, given the groundcover and mucky puddles. Another boot print—Brown's, this time—led them to the edge of the bog where the ground grew firmer and sloped gently upward to meet the woods.

They paused at the edge of the trees, looking for snapped twigs, scuffled dirt or any other indication of the way Brown and Laney had gone. The rising sun peeked through the leaves far above, dappling the ground with bright light. He strained to hear anything beyond the noisy morning chorus of birds, but there was nothing out of place.

Tapping Henderson's shoulder, he nodded toward what might be a narrow trail leading south-southeast. A crumpled seedling looked freshly crushed, making hope spring into his chest. This would go faster if they called in a dog, but Ryan didn't want to run the risk of being overheard unless he had to.

Because if Brown heard them coming, hard on his heels…

Ryan didn't want to imagine how a desperate killer might act in that situation. Instead, he sucked in a calming breath and gestured for Henderson to follow him down the trail.

Laney couldn't stop her hands from shaking. She'd agreed to this plan—no, scratch that—the plan was *her* idea. But she hadn't expected fear to take over her body like this, an all-consuming, gut-churning terror that drove her blindly forward through the trees.

Brown didn't even have a physical weapon out, and yet here she was, stumbling and scurrying in front of him as if his sickening grin held her at gunpoint. But that was where a serial killer's power came from, wasn't it? From the victim's own sense of horror, the way her body had turned against her. And the fact that they both knew someone else's life was at stake.

Laney had walked into this trap willingly to save a girl she didn't know, and even if she could escape now, she wouldn't. Not with another life on the line.

How far had they walked since he'd ripped the tracker off her stomach and tossed it into the water? Did Ryan know? Was he coming behind them, ready to intervene the second they found the other victim?

Or...maybe he was still in the field, scouring the bog for any trace of her, trying to pick up her trail. Lawrence Brown had evaded capture for years, even succeeded in sending a supposed friend to jail in his place. He knew the cops would come; maybe he had a plan to give them the slip.

Maybe Ryan wouldn't make it in time.

Her heart squeezed hard at the thought, and she forced out a tiny prayer for help. Hope. Peace. The kind of prayer spoken in groans rather than true words.

Jesus had promised to be with her always. Nothing could separate her from His love—not even Brown's breath blowing hot against the back of her neck as he took her arm. He steered her off the path they'd been following and down a short incline. Over what looked like a narrow drainage ditch and then back up the other side.

Realization dawned on her as a dark tumbledown cabin came into view between the trees. Old man Waltman, the bog's namesake, had built a cabin back in these woods a hundred years earlier. Rumor claimed the place had been abandoned for nearly thirty years. When she was in high school, the kids sometimes dared each other to go searching for the cabin at night, but to her knowledge, nobody ever had.

"Home sweet home," Brown said, surveying her with a frenzied gleam in his eyes.

Nerves made her throat close, but she forced herself to breathe. "This isn't your property."

"Actually, it is." He smiled. "You might call it a family inheritance."

Was he a descendent of Waltman? Or had he finagled the land out of somebody else somewhere down the line? Laney supposed it didn't matter. Not when he was dragging her toward the door to take her inside and kill her. The roof, sagging at one time, had been shored up with new lumber on the far end. But the cracked windows were missing glass in places and the faded exterior planking was weathered and splitting.

"Is this where you brought the others?" she asked as he pulled the solid wood door open. It rattled on the hinges. Was this the last place Jenna was alive?

"See for yourself."

Her stomach dropped as she glanced around the dark interior. A lone chair stood in the center of the floorboards, the girl from the photograph tied to it. Her eyes were wide, and she whimpered beneath the silver duct tape covering her mouth. Dried blood curled in two sweeping arcs across each cheek.

The rest of the cabin was bare save for an empty hearth and a long table against the wall. Above it hung a collection of rusty tools—blunt-ended hammers and screwdrivers and jagged saw blades, the metal contrasting starkly against the fading yellow paint of the clapboard wall. Any one of them could be responsible for the damage she'd found on the victims' bones.

Laney shuddered as Brown pulled the door shut behind them.

But now wasn't the time to collapse under the weight of fear. Now was the time to bargain for that poor girl who didn't have anything to do with this case, who had ended up in the wrong place at the wrong time. The same way as Jenna.

Please, Lord, protect her. And help me be strong.

She nodded toward the woman. "Let her go. You only have one chair, and I'm the one you wanted."

Brown smiled as his cheeks flushed, the expression all the more terrifying because of the possessive warmth in his eyes. "I've wanted you in this cabin since the moment I heard you were coming back, no matter what *she* had to say about it."

"She?"

"My meddlesome... Never you mind." His hand clenched, and for a moment Laney thought he might kill both her and Madison Smith. But then he dragged Laney over to the chair, stopping in front of the other victim and pulling a knife from the recesses of his pocket.

"It's your special day," he said, his tone almost hysterically happy. "This pretty lady has volunteered to take your place." He cut the ropes tying her to the chair. As soon as she was free, she rose on unsteady legs, duct tape still stretched across her face.

Laney held her breath as he grabbed the girl's arm to escort her—

Not to the front door, but to a door on the left side of

the fireplace. She clenched her teeth so hard tears sprang into her eyes. Had she given herself up for nothing?

"You can wait in here," Brown said gruffly as he shoved her into what looked like a bedroom. "Just in case Laney tries anything."

His back was to Laney—maybe now was her best chance to escape. Ryan had to be close. They could get back here and save Madison before it was too late. The far window, with the pane partially broken out, would be the best bet. If she could get to it fast enough.

But as she took a single, hesitating step toward it, Brown turned. His expression fell, the downturned pout of his lips revoltingly childlike.

Laney froze.

"Don't leave, Laney. I planned this all out just for you."

Her heart lurched as he stepped toward her, his knife waving carelessly in the air. If she lunged for the window, could she make it in time?

No, not with those razor-edged shards jutting from the window frame. Even if she risked slicing her arms open, the broken part wasn't big enough to fit through. She'd have to bust out more of the glass, and Brown wouldn't move *that* slow.

She pressed her lips together and inhaled a couple of deep breaths through her nose as he held out a hand toward the now-empty chair. Ryan wouldn't stop looking for her, even without the help of the tracker. If she could just buy him enough time, he'd find them. Brown would get the justice he deserved.

Her legs felt like wooden blocks as she shuffled to the chair, jerking away from Brown's outstretched hand as he tried to help her sit. "Don't touch me," she snapped, fear tinting the anger in her tone. "You promised you'd let that girl go."

"I haven't broken my word...yet." Brown's lips tilted again as he picked the rope up off the floor, thick fingers caressing the smooth coils. He draped the rope around her arms and chest, looping it around the back of the chair, leaning in close enough that Laney could smell spiced aftershave mingled with body odor. Her nose crinkled as a chill tracked across her shoulders.

Brown smiled wider, inhaling deeply through his nose. As if he were breathing in her terror. But it was all about power with serial killers, wasn't it? "I've looked forward to this moment for a long time." He finished tying the rope and stood back, surveying her.

His words cracked through the panic buzzing in her brain, and she frowned. "Then why did you plant the bomb in my suitcase? Or the police chief's house?"

"Not my idea."

"What about framing Ronald Wilson? Was that your idea?"

His rough laughter echoed in the still room. "That was my sister Kathleen's. Never knew when to mind her own business. Shame about Ron. He was our friend. Besides, that was a lot of trouble for nothin'." He crouched in front of Laney, something manic flickering through his eyes. "I'm far more interested in other things than disposing of evidence."

Her breath froze in her lungs as he stretched the knife toward her face and pressed the cold flat side of the blade against her skin. Fear rose like an animal inside her chest, clawing against her ribs and throat, struggling to escape. *Please, Lord. Let them find me in time.* And if not...

Give me strength.

"Why—" her voice cracked, and she struggled to clear it "—why did you kill the first one ten years ago? The girl on the bike?"

Brown pulled the knife back and tilted his head to one side, his eyes softening in a mockery of her emotions. "You know the answer. Don't you, Laney?" He stared, waiting for her to say something, but Laney's entire mouth and throat had frozen shut.

Brown's eyes followed the rise and fall of her throat as she swallowed, struggling to get some moisture back into her mouth. Her. He'd meant to kill *her*.

"That's right, Laney. I didn't care about that other girl. *You* were the one I wanted, to get back at Kim. You two biked near my house all the time. I watched every day, waiting for an opening, and when I saw you stopped on the side of the road, fixing the bike…"

"But it wasn't me." As if protesting now could bring Jenna back.

"No, it wasn't." His hard eyes glittered with cruelty. "All that time I'd waited, and it wasn't you. But she was small and powerless, and I was angry enough to kill." He stared down at his hands almost wistfully, apparently lost in the memory, and a shudder rippled up Laney's back.

"Why the others?" Her voice came out in a ragged whisper.

He shrugged. Careless. "After that, I *knew*. I knew what if felt like to take a life. And I had to feel that power again. Kathleen tried to make me stop after Wilson went to jail, but…I can't. And you skipped town so fast, I never got another chance with you. Until now." A wicked smile curled his lips.

She shrank against the back of the chair, cold terror raising goose bumps on her arms. She darted her gaze across the windows, hoping to see movement flickering outside.

But there were only the fluttering of green leaves on the trees and Brown's words drifting through her haze of fear.

"Now it's your turn, Laney."

EIGHTEEN

Laney closed her eyes, inhaling a shaky breath as a prayer without words flung itself up to heaven. She waited for the cold, biting press of steel against her skin.

It couldn't end this way, not after everything she and Ryan had gone through. Not when she hadn't gotten the chance to tell him how much she still loved him.

A loud creak sounded from behind her, and she cranked her head to the left in time to see an interior door slide open. Not the one to the room containing Madison Smith but the one on the other side of the hearth.

A gun emerged first, held at arm's length by someone wearing a police uniform.

Officer Sarah McIntosh.

Relief cascaded through Laney until she slumped like a rag doll against the ropes tying her to the chair. Praise God.

"Freeze." Sarah stopped ten feet away, the gun aimed at Brown's head. No German shepherd stood at attention nearby. She must've broken in through a back window and had to leave Marty outside.

Did that mean Ryan and the others were outside too? Hope buoyed Laney's chest—

Until she glanced at Lawrence Brown's face and saw the way his lips curled.

"Sarah, what are you doin' here?" He pointed the knife at her. "You got no business interfering."

Laney's mouth dropped open. She snapped it shut, glancing between them. "Sarah?"

Brown smiled again. "I believe you've met my daughter, Sarah *Brown* McIntosh."

Sarah's face contorted into a grimace. "I'm sorry, Laney. I really am. I never wanted you to get involved or for things to go so far. All I wanted was to scare you off before you figured out the truth."

"*You're* the bomber?" Laney could barely choke out the words. And yet it made perfect sense. Sarah would know exactly how to make a pipe bomb. How to plant the materials in someone else's garage. And where to find Laney at nearly every given moment, thanks to her inside knowledge of the police department. "But...you were with us at his house. You never—"

"—acted like we were related?" Sarah laughed bitterly. "I'd forget the relationship entirely if his name weren't on my birth certificate."

"Why didn't Ted Kincaide recognize you?" Laney pressed.

"Why would he? His ex-wife might be my aunt, but my mom kept me from this side of the family as much as possible. Jasper, remember? It wasn't until college that I got the hare-brained notion of trying to build a relationship with my father. *That* was a mistake." Her eyes narrowed at Brown.

Pity pricked at Laney's insides. She and Sarah had more in common than she'd guessed. How would she feel if she learned her missing father was someone like

Lawrence Brown? And yet…she'd *never* help a killer. "I still don't understand. Why not turn him in?"

"Ha," she scoffed. "I'd think you of all people with your junkie mom would understand? I mean, you high-tailed it out of here soon as you could." Something in her eyes shifted. "But how would you like everyone knowing your father was a serial killer? That dear old Dad had been murdering and dismembering women for a decade, and you'd been too chicken to turn him in when you first overheard him and your aunt discussing where to hide a body, so now technically you were an accomplice?" She had that wild-animal look. "How about the fact that you'd never mentioned this information to your employer or the love of your life?" Her eyes went cold. "Somehow I don't think that would go over very well."

Lawrence Brown flipped the knife around in his hand, shifting his weight from one leg to the other. "Get lost, Sarah. You shouldn't have interfered."

"Drop the knife," she insisted, inching closer with her gun still on his head.

"Or what?" Brown laughed mirthlessly. "*Now* you're going to play good cop and turn me in? Isn't it a little late for that?"

"No, it's not," Laney interrupted. "Sarah, it's never too late to make the right decision."

"Of course it's too late," Sarah snapped. "Don't be naive. If you would've just taken the next flight out, I would've had more time to find a way to safely destroy those bones before they were studied. Even now, I can still try to make the evidence inadmissible in court."

She glared at her father. "But not with *you* around. If you would've just stayed out of it and let me deal with her instead of playing your twisted games, we wouldn't be in this mess."

Brown scowled. "Your cop friends will be here any minute. Whatever you're planning, it won't erase the fact that they'll know I was involved. You'll never be free of me."

"On the contrary..." Sarah tugged a messenger bag over her head, then lowered it gingerly to the ground a few paces from Laney's chair. She crouched beside it and reached inside to fiddle with something. "I planted enough evidence at Kathleen's to make sure she and Ted look guilty."

She pulled a length of rope from her utility belt. "And there'll be too little of you left to identify. Now get behind the chair."

Brown held up both hands, the knife dangling loosely in one palm. "Now, surely you want to rethink this, sweetheart. Ain't no reason you can't let me out of this cabin before you blow it."

"Wrong." Sarah's jaw clenched as she approached Brown, the gun level in one hand, the rope loose in the other. "See that bag over there? I already activated the bomb, just to make sure this mess gets cleaned up one way or another. That last cell phone detonation was too risky. This time we're going the old-fashioned way—a timer."

There'd be a moment where she'd have to lower her weapon to tie up Brown, and in that instant, Laney would have to do *something*. She had no clue what, but she wasn't about to sit here and let someone blow her up. Or that poor college girl either.

"How many minutes?" Her voice came out as a high-pitched squeak.

"Enough for me to get out into the woods and join the search crew." She waved the rope at Brown. "Now drop your weapon and get behind her."

He kept the knife but circled slowly around Laney until he stood directly to her right. Sarah advanced a few more feet on Laney's left, wedging her in the middle of their standoff. She wrapped trembling fingers around the hard edges of the wooden seat, shifting her weight ever so slightly to test the balance. The thing wobbled—not much, but it would be enough.

She hoped.

Sarah took another step closer, until Laney could've reached out and touched the muzzle of her gun if her arms weren't tied. "I said drop the knife."

Brown hesitated as if weighing his chances. Sarah was law enforcement—she couldn't miss at this range—but Brown had that manic look in his eye again, like a trapped animal. And Laney was caught right in between them.

Nobody breathed until Brown finally started to crouch, lowering the knife. Moving at a snail's pace.

Sarah lifted the coiled rope. "You're going to kneel behind that chair, and I'm going to tie your hands to it. Nice and easy, and I won't need to shoot."

"Sure, darlin'. Whatever you say." Brown smirked. The same way he'd looked during the police interrogation—like he knew he was going to win.

The knife scraped across the ground as Brown crept around her. When he'd made it to the back, Laney shifted in her seat again—gently, so that hopefully neither of them would notice.

As Sarah edged closer, Laney rocked a little harder. *Please, God, let this work. Keep me safe.*

Brown made his move when Sarah was within leaping distance, bursting out from behind the chair and launching himself at her knees.

Laney jerked to her right with all her strength, sending

the seat toppling sideways as a gunshot blasted through the confined space.

Her shoulder slammed into the wood, and she strained to keep her head from crashing down too. Sharp pain lanced up through her arm from the hand crushed beneath the seat edge, making tears spring into her eyes.

Grunts and thumps sounded from behind her, the other two fighting where she could no longer see them. The gun must've missed its mark. She strained against the ropes, trying to work her left arm out of the bindings.

The cabin grew still as the sounds of struggling ceased. She held her breath, waiting to see who'd won. Was it too much to hope they'd both died?

Footsteps thudded across the floor. Too heavy to be Sarah.

She tensed as Lawrence Brown walked into view. He stopped in front of her, cocking his head to one side as he dragged his knife blade across his shirt, leaving a long smear of blood. "A real pity, Laney. I never wanted to hurt her. Not my own flesh and blood. You, though…"

The bomb. *What about the bomb?* The question formed in her mind, but she couldn't force it onto her numb tongue as he heaved her chair back upright. The messenger bag still lay on the floor ten feet away, just past Sarah McIntosh's body, now lying motionless in a pool of blood from a knife wound to the chest.

None of that mattered as Brown raised the knife to Laney's cheek.

Ryan paused outside the cabin, listening intently. He and Henderson had been close when they'd heard the gunshot, close enough the sound led them the rest of the way. He desperately hoped it wasn't Laney.

Please, God, let us get to her on time. Surely Brown wouldn't shoot her, not after going to all this trouble.

He tapped his mic rapidly in their prearranged code. Three quick taps. Pause. Two taps. Pause. One.

The tech's voice issued softly through his earpiece. *"Copy that, Sergeant Mitchell. Backup teams are en route to your location. ETA five minutes. Also, I have a message from Officer McIntosh. Kathleen Kincaide is your bomber. Her dog alerted at Kincaide's home, but Kathleen wasn't there. She put an APB out to find the suspect."*

Ryan tapped his mic again to let her know he'd received the message. So, Ted Kincaide had been telling the truth—his ex-wife had framed him. But where was she now? Waiting inside that cabin to dispose of Laney's body?

Wherever she was, five minutes was too long to wait. He gritted his teeth and leaned in toward Henderson, speaking in a barely audible whisper. "Backup ETA five minutes. I'm going in the front. You cover me."

The other man nodded and signaled toward a clump of trees opposite the clearing from the cabin's door. Ryan gave him a thumbs-up and scrambled down into the drainage ditch as Henderson worked his way around the clearing.

Ryan paused again at the last bit of cover before the trees gave way to open grass. He'd have to cross maybe thirty feet of space before reaching the cabin wall. The only window facing his direction had a pane partially broken out.

The thumping he'd heard had stopped, replaced now by the low rumble of a man's voice.

He watched for a moment, but no face appeared behind the cracked glass. If he worked his way through the brush a bit farther toward the back of the cabin, he'd be less likely to be seen when he crossed the clearing. But the noise might alert the man inside to his presence, and the last thing Ryan wanted was to lose Laney now, when help was so close.

Easing his gun from its holster, he released the safety and ducked low as he raced across the open grass. The interior of the cabin had gone silent by the time he reached the decaying logs beneath the damaged panes.

He crept around the front corner of the cabin, keeping low beneath the front window until he reached the door. The tech's voice came through his earpiece. *"Three teams moving in on your location. No sign of the other victim yet."*

Slipping past the cabin's door, he stood on the far side, pressing his back against the wall. The door's lock appeared to be a simple latch, one that would break with a single gunshot. Across the clearing, Henderson saluted. The other officers would be in position any minute.

Aiming his gun at the lock, Ryan fired. He grabbed the rough edge of the heavy door, pulling it open far enough to kick it the rest of the way. Gun extended, he stood partially in the doorway, using the cabin wall as a shield.

His chest seized as his eyes adjusted enough to see inside the gloomy cabin.

Lawrence Brown turned to look at him, a blood-coated knife in his hand, red slathered across his shirt. And in the chair behind him—

Laney.

She blinked at him, dark hair all messy and cheeks pale but—praise God—still alive and with no sign of blood. Then whose…?

Wait—another body lay on the floor close by, unrecognizable from this angle except for the police uniform. A dull ache spread across his chest. Who'd gotten here first? And why hadn't they called for backup?

"I wouldn't come any closer if I were you," Brown said lazily. He flashed the knife and with his other hand held up a black handgun. "Otherwise I'll have to shoot her."

"This isn't going to end the way you think," Ryan said. "We've got the cabin surrounded. Give yourself up, and nobody needs to get hurt."

"Ryan—" the trembling in Laney's voice nearly broke his heart "—there's a bomb. In that bag." She tipped her head toward a dark shape on the floor on the far side of the body. "I don't know how much time we have."

Brown smirked at Ryan before turning back to her. "Then you and I can be together in death, Laney." His knife clattered to the floor as he switched the gun to his other hand.

"Drop the gun, Brown!" Ryan commanded, fear edging its way into his voice. He couldn't take the shot from here, not with Laney right behind. At this distance, the bullet might pass through and hit her.

He took a step through the doorway, planning to edge his way into the room, but Brown raised the arm with the gun. Ryan's insides twisted as the firearm lifted closer to Laney's forehead.

A sharp crack sent his heart up into his throat until Brown crumpled to the ground. *Henderson.* Praise God. The other officer withdrew his gun from the broken window at the end of the cabin and saluted Ryan.

Ryan rushed into the cabin, issuing orders into his mic. "Ten-ninety-nine. Officer down. Ten-eighty-seven. Bomb in the cabin. Keep back." He swiped a knife from his utility belt and cut Laney free. The warmth in her eyes threatened to steal his breath, but they didn't have the luxury to talk yet.

"Madison Smith is trapped in there." She pointed to one of the doors behind her with her left hand, clutching the other to her chest as he escorted her toward the entrance.

"I'll get her." Ryan passed her off to Henderson before dashing back inside. The interior door was unlocked. He found the student inside, slumped against the wall and shivering. In shock, no doubt. Speaking in soothing tones, he helped her up off the ground and hurried her out through the entrance.

He stopped after handing her off to another officer, allowing himself one last glance at Laney. She sat on a fallen tree at the far edge of the clearing, still clutching that hand to her chest. Her dark eyes followed his every movement.

No time now to think about all the things he still wanted to say. Instead, he raised his hand, tore away his gaze and turned back into the cabin.

The bomb had to be in that bag on the ground. He dashed first to the fallen officer, spending a precious second to check for signs of life despite the pool of blood. It was Officer Sarah McIntosh. She was gone. Stab wound to the chest. But why was she here? Because of this bomb?

Confusion and grief twisted beneath his ribs, but there was no time for questions now. Praying this moment wouldn't be his last, he gingerly lifted the bag's flap.

A bright red timer flashed the countdown. Three minutes.

Praise the Lord, there was time. But not much. With Sarah gone, they needed their other bomb tech.

"Ten-seventy-five. Johnson. I need Johnson ASAP. Three minutes and counting down."

Laney held her breath as she listened to Ryan's voice crackling over the nearest officer's radio. More had arrived on the scene now, including Cam, the one who'd recognized her at the bog. Her hand throbbed so badly she could barely concentrate on the blur of motion and noise around her.

An officer rushed into the cabin to help Ryan. *Please, God, please...*

The next moments were almost as painful as her aching body. Waiting, unable to help, wondering if the cabin would blow and take the evidence and the one true love of her life with it.

Then all Laney could see was Ryan jogging out the front door and crouching down in front of her, his beautiful dark eyes gleaming with hope and concern, his lips slightly open as if he wanted to speak but couldn't quite find the words.

All the fear she'd kept back during the last hours crumbled, dissolving into a well of emotion that could find an outlet only through tears. Thankfulness to be alive. Gratitude for God's justice and mercy.

And a joy and longing so intense she couldn't put it in words. She and Ryan still had a chance to figure out what God wanted them to be. Smiling, she struggled to blink away the tears.

"Hey," he said, his voice heartbreakingly gentle. He brushed his fingertips lightly against her cheek. "You okay?"

"Yeah." The word resounded deep through her insides. Because the truth was, she hadn't felt okay for a long time. Not for at least ten years. But now God had brought her back here, to face everything she'd run away from, to find justice for Jenna and to see Ryan. "I am."

He stared at her a moment longer, dark eyebrows pulling together as if he recognized the weight of years behind her words. Then his eyes caught on the injured hand she still cradled against her chest. "Hey, let me take a look at that."

She held it out, the fingers curled in like a dead spider's legs. The back of her hand had turned into a dark, swollen mass. "I think I broke a couple of metacarpals when I tipped the chair over."

"Metacarpals?" When he quirked an eyebrow, she launched into a recount of what had happened, his expression falling when she got to the part about Sarah McIntosh.

"That's why she's inside." He dragged a hand over his face. "Laney, I'm so sorry. But now it makes sense. Sarah wanted to keep Brown's identity as the killer hidden, so she threatened you at the airport and convinced Brown to plant the bomb in your suitcase. But as soon as Brown realized who you were, he picked you as his next victim."

Laney nodded. "Sarah tried to incriminate Ted Kincaide once Lawrence gave up the location of the truck, and she planted the bomb at your house in another attempt to scare me off."

"When all of it failed," he added, "she faked a visit to Kathleen's and came here instead. Though we'll still arrest Kathleen for framing Wilson." He held out his hand, and she marveled at how perfectly hers fit against his palm. "Here, let me help you up."

Her legs wobbled for a moment as she regained her balance, and Ryan's expression clouded. "I'm okay," she insisted. "Ryan, we did it. The Sandy Bluff serial killer is gone, Jenna will have justice and you'll have all the evidence you need. Was Madison Smith all right?"

"She's okay, thanks to you. What you did was incredibly brave, Laney."

Heat made her cheeks flush at his praise. "I couldn't have done it without you."

"Let's get you some medical attention." He wrapped an arm around her back.

But her feet wouldn't cooperate, not when words sat heavy inside her heart. She'd kept them tucked away long enough. "Ryan, wait."

When he stopped and faced her, his brown eyes melting like chocolate, she found it suddenly hard to breathe.

"What is it?"

"I…" Her mouth went dry, the words sticking despite their eagerness to escape. "I wanted to tell you earlier. I *should* have told you." She paused to swallow, and a trace of a frown crinkled his brow.

"What?"

"I love you. I've loved you for as long as I can remember, and ten years apart did nothing to change the way I feel." The weight lifted off her chest, and her lips tilted up on one side almost on their own. "Other than to make me love you more."

"Laney…" His voice was thick, his expression a mixture of happiness and hope and disbelief. "I don't know what I would've done if I'd lost you."

He pulled her against his chest, being careful of her injured hand, but she could sense the fierce intensity kept at bay by his gentleness.

"Thank God He had different plans for us," she said,

her words muffled by his starchy uniform shirt and the hard flak jacket underneath.

Relaxing his grip, Ryan held her out enough to study her face. "Laney, I could never ask you to come back here. I know how much you've suffered in this place."

Her heart swelled at his thoughtfulness. "I would consider it, though, if it meant being with you."

His lips pressed warm and firm against her forehead. When he pulled away to look at her again, his gaze burned. "I know you would, but it wouldn't be right. It's okay if you want to take things slowly and see what happens. But—" his eyebrows quirked, adorably cute in their hopefulness "—if you'll have me, I'll leave Sandy Bluff and move to DC with you. I would've asked you to marry me ten years ago if I'd known I might never get another chance."

"Are you asking now?" Her voice was breathless, her heart giddy with joy. How did emotions flip-flop like this, from fear of imminent death to life-changing happiness within the span of half an hour?

"Yes." He glanced at the pine-needle strewn ground. "I'd get down on one knee if I thought you wouldn't collapse."

Her lips split into a wide grin. "Not necessary. I just hope Jenna can see us from heaven. She'd be so happy."

He nodded, his expression one of bittersweet joy. "Is that a yes, then?"

"Of course it's a yes! Ryan Mitchell, you've always been my other half. It just took a long detour before I realized it."

The warmth in his eyes melted away the adrenaline coursing through her system, replacing it with heady anticipation. He leaned in to kiss her—their first real kiss in a decade, and yet the years felt like they'd vanished.

From the corner of her eye, she noticed an officer stop a few feet away. "Everything okay over here…?" Cam's voice died away until he coughed. "Apparently so."

Laney and Ryan laughed, and he turned to Cam. "She just, uh, needs to get checked out."

"Looks like you got the 'checked-out' part covered, Sergeant." Cam snickered.

Laney's gaze locked on Ryan's, and twin grins formed. He cleared his throat. "I mean, from a medical professional."

Was that a blush working its way up into his cheeks? She winked at him, and he winked back. "Lead me away then, Sergeant Mitchell."

Morning sunlight streamed into the clearing, warm and comforting on Laney's face as Ryan guided her out from under the trees. Other officers had started the painstaking task of documenting all the evidence.

Laney lifted a hand in question. "I can get a ride with someone else if you need to stay and oversee the work?"

Ryan's lips quirked. "Right. As if I'm ever leaving your side again."

She roped her arm through his, smiling up at him, and together they took the first steps into the joyful new life that lay ahead.

EPILOGUE

Eighteen months later

Ryan winced as Laney squeezed his hand so tightly his wedding ring dug into his fingers. She lay back against the hospital bed, panting, her face lined with exhaustion. Yet her eyes had never looked more alive as a tiny cry pierced the room.

"Great job, sweetheart. I'm so proud of you," he said, squeezing her hand back and glancing anxiously at the doctor. Despite years in the police force and now a year on the streets of Washington, DC, he'd never been in a more stressful situation than this moment, when the two loves of his life hung in the balance.

"Congratulations." The doctor smiled, softening her normally stern expression. She held out a wriggling little red bundle of moving limbs. "It's a girl! And she's perfect."

Laney laughed, pure delight written across her features, as the doctor handed their daughter to her.

A girl.

Ryan's throat burned, and he turned his face to one side in a probably pointless effort to hide the water pooling in his eyes. Despite all his mistakes and all the tragedy he and Laney had endured, God had given them a second chance. Both to accept His love and to find this joy with each other. And now they were parents.

"It's okay." Laney's warm fingers found his arm, and he looked back at her, blinking furiously. "You can cry. It'll only make me love you more."

He leaned over, pressing a kiss to her forehead. Then another on the downy, impossibly soft black hair of his newborn daughter. "A girl. My mother isn't going to leave us alone."

Laney turned the baby around so he could see her full face. Her little eyes opened, revealing lovely dark brown irises, and she blinked slowly at him. Ryan's heart threatened to burst right out of his chest.

"She's more beautiful than I could possibly have imagined," he said, the words catching on unshed tears.

Laney kissed the little head. "Yes, she is."

"Do you have a name picked out?" One of the nurses asked, her eyes bright.

He exchanged a glance with Laney, who nodded.

"Yeah." The burning in his throat made it hard to speak, and he had to blink again to clear his blurring vision. "Her name is Jenna Elaine Mitchell."

Laney smiled up at him, her gaze filled with love and wonder and the promise of all God's good blessings still to come.

* * * * *

If you enjoyed Buried Evidence, *pick up this other thrilling story from Kellie VanHorn:*

Fatal Flashback

Available now from Love Inspired Suspense!
Find more great reads at www.LoveInspired.com

Dear Reader,

This story was difficult for me to write. Maybe because I worked on it during the lockdown, maybe because it was a second book, but most likely because it was inspired by an actual disappearance that happened in my college town years ago, on the same roads I had biked in my spare time.

Grappling with loss is one of the hardest parts of life on this earth. I can't tell you how comforting it is to know that God is always with us and that even when we face the worst, we won't do it alone. Our souls rest secure in His strong hands, and someday He will make all things right.

Thank you so much for taking this journey with me. I love hearing from readers, so please feel free to get in touch with me through my website, www.kellievanhorn.com.

Warm regards,
Kellie VanHorn